Song of Siwa

Song of Siwa

The Marzuk-Iskander Festival

Siwa Oasis, Western Desert,

Arab Republic of Egypt

Author: Louis Grivetti
Artist: Alison Smith

Library of Congress Control Number: 2013913427
ISBN: Hardcover   978-1-4836-7268-7
               Softcover   978-1-4836-7267-0
               Ebook   978-1-4836-7269-4

Cover image credits:

1. Bathing in the Sun's Well [Taut es-Shamps], 1969.
   Artist: Refaat Ahmed
   Photograph: Louis Grivetti, 2013
   Author's private collection

2. Siwa Girl, 1969.
   Artist: Refaat Ahmed
   Photograph: Louis Grivetti, 2013
   Author's private collection

3. Siwa Girls, 1969
   Artist: Refaat Ahmed
   Photograph: Louis Grivetti, 2013
   Author's private collection

Rev. date: 08/07/2013

To order additional copies of this book, contact:
Xlibris LLC
1-888-795-4274
www.Xlibris.com
Orders@Xlibris.com
136973

Table of Contents

Part 3: After Notes

Appendices:

Dedication

To the memory of my friend Ibrahim Helmi who guided members of our team to safety after the accident to our vehicles in the Qattara Depression near Bir abd al-Nebi during the expedition to Siwa and Qara oasis, spring 1966.

Acknowledgments

I wish to thank . . .

Alison Smith for her creative and distinctive art work that added substance and character to *The Song of Siwa*;

Dr. Paul Haverkamp for preparing the satellite photographs and Steve Oerding for rendering the finished maps that accompany the text;

Axel Borg, Georgette Grivetti, Dr. Paul Haverkamp, Thurber Reynolds, Dr. Margaret Swisher, and Dr. Megan Wyman for comments and suggestions that improved the original draft manuscript;

Special thanks to the Xlibris team members who provided assistance and advice during the publishing and post-production process: Pamela Blake, Post Publication Supervisor; Faith Go, Submission Representative; Vanessa Marzo, Supervisor Customer Satisfaction; Jaysee Pingkian, Production Specialist; David Ross, Post Publication Representative; Amy Scott, Author Services Representative; Stephen Verona, Senior Publishing Consultant; and Orlando Wade, Marketing Service Representative.

Most of all I wish to thank the residents of Siwa and Qara oases who provided hospitality and assistance to me during my visits in 1965 and 1966—and who served as the inspiration for *The Song of Siwa*.

Louis Grivetti
Davis, California
2013

Preface

The oasis of Siwa—a geographical jewel of safe haven and wonder—lies in the Western Desert of Egypt. History records that in 332 BCE Alexander the Great visited the oasis and its renowned oracle temple. The purpose of his visit was to seek knowledge regarding his conception—whether his father was human or divine. For more than 2000 years at 15 year intervals the oasis residents have convened a festival [*mulid*] to honor the memory and name of the young Macedonian King who they call *Iskander: al-Kahana Thalthe* [Alexander: The Third Priest]. The central component of the ceremony is the formal recitation of an epic story, said to have been composed within a century after Alexander's death in 323 BCE, perhaps during the reign of Ptolemy III (Euergetes) who ruled Egypt between 246-222 BCE.

The Song of Siwa, also known as The Marzuk-Iskander Epic, is chanted as a key part of the desert festival. The style reflects the North African and Middle Eastern style, structure, and tone of oral traditions passed down through the centuries as told and re-told at festivals and social gatherings. The epic story is chanted by a team of five respected elders who have memorized the words as taught to them by a hereditary line of male relatives. It is possible that these elders are part of a continuous chain of speakers that may date back more than two millennia. The Egyptian folklore scholar Atif al-Barzan attempted an Arabic transcription and translation of the epic, a version that circulated locally in Cairo shortly after the 1905 *mulid*.[1] His version, however, omitted significant sections of the epic for reasons that are unclear.

My objective in presenting and publishing the present work has been to honor the spirit of the festival and the Marzuk-Iskander epic and to respect the wishes of Siwi elders who urged me long ago to share their oral traditions and history with others. My translation of *The Song of Siwa* is based upon my field notes and tape recordings made at the time of the 1965 *mulid*. Scholars may examine these original materials that currently are deposited in the archive section of the Egyptian Desert Research Library, #38 Sharia Kasr al-Nile, Cairo, Egypt [Document File: 27-B-1965]. Formal inquiries to inspect the documents should be made to the Director, Dr. Ismael al-Shami; letters of introduction along with academic and professional credentials should accompany each request.

Initial passages of the epic relate the exploits of the hero Marzuk who led his stone-age clan of hunters from their original home in central Iberia (modern Spain) across the Mediterranean Sea to safety in Africa, a perilous journey on pine-log rafts during the last Ice Age, perhaps c. 10,000 BCE. Passages of the chant suggest that the voyagers reached the general region of what is now west-coastal Algeria.

The next sequence of verses chronicle the clan's trans-Saharan trek south and ultimately east through what currently are the al-Haggar and al-Air regions of the central Sahara. At the time of Marzuk's passage this geographical area would have been a lush well-watered zone filled with wild game, not the arid desert that it is today in the 21st century. The hunters continued their eastward migration following game herds until they reached the mountains of Tibesti and ultimately crossed through the undulating dune zone now called the Great Sand Sea to reach safe haven at Siwa oasis located in the Western Desert of modern Egypt.

The middle verses document the clan's genealogy and the names and activities of subsequent leaders and describe how the once unified hunters ultimately split into two separate clan divisions, one remaining at Siwa and the second occupying Qara, a small oasis located east of Siwa situated along the western edge of the vast Qattara Depression. The two clan segments subsequently were reunified after Tella King of Qara defeated Ferzin King of the Siwa in a climatic death duel.

Then follow verses that relate the tenuous political and social relationships between the Siwans and adjacent Libyan tribes and successive periods of peace and conflict between the Siwan/Libyan allies and the Chemi—peoples of the Black Land—inhabitants of the ancient Nile Valley. The epic documents years of trial when the Siwan/Libyan alliance was defeated twice by superior Chemi military tactics, events that resulted in Chemi occupation and rule over Siwa.

The latter epic verses include descriptions of the Persian military invasion of the Nile Valley Black Land and the harsh occupation and rule of King Cambyses. This section also relates the disastrous Persian military expedition to attack Siwa from the south and key passages provide the basis for events that led to the annihilation Persian forces by sandstorm.

The remaining verses document the early exploits of Alexander the Great and his welcome invasion of the Black Land. These components set the stage for the young general's decision to visit the oracle temple of Amon-Ra at Siwa oasis. This portion of the epic concludes with Alexander's untimely death at Babylon and the return of his body to Egypt where the Macedonian King initially was buried at the newly constructed coastal city of Alexandria.

The epic ends with verses that consider the mysterious disappearance of Alexander's body and reconfirm the return of his protective spirit to the Siwa, where he has been celebrated in name and tradition for more than 2,000 years as the Third Priest [al-Kahana Thalthet].

How I learned about the festival and my decision to travel to Siwa to attend the 1965 mulid, is presented here in the initial pages. After a short introduction my translation of the epic follows.

Louis Grivetti
Davis, California
2013

---

1. al-Barzan, Atif. 1906. Al-Kash Milhmyh Marzukaya [The Marzuk Saga]. Cairo, Egypt: Dar al-Sheffa Publishers. 77 pages.

PART 1

Prelude

Introduction

The story begins upon my arrival in Egypt during early August, 1964. I was part of a team of American and Egyptian researchers assembled to investigate emerging diet- and health-related problems among Awlad Ali Bedouins who had abandoned their nomadic lifestyle and settled in coastal lands west of Alexandria. While conducting fieldwork at the villages of Bahig and Hammam, I occasionally heard fragments of information regarding an interesting *mulid,* or festival/ceremony, held occasionally at Siwa oasis. One of my Bedouin assistants, Belhag ibn Musa abd al-Karim, had visited Siwa as a child prior to World War II. He had accompanied his father and uncle when they had driven their herds of sheep south across the desert plateau into the well-watered oasis to escape the drought that had ravaged their north-coast grazing areas. Belhag informed me that he had been too young to attend or participate in the *mulid,* but that his father had related some of the events that had taken place. Gradually, I learned that the Third Priest festival was real and not just a myth to excite the imagination. At the same time it also seemed curious to me that such an event attracted little regional attention outside of Siwa oasis as none of my Egyptian friends in Cairo had even heard of the festival.

During February 1965, contacts informed me that the *mulid* would be held two months later in April. Since there was a lull in my work I decided to visit Siwa and attend the festivities. At the same time, I recognized that my decision lay more in the realm of adventure than in seeking truth and cultural understanding. When I declared my intent to my friends in Cairo all shook their heads in disbelief and most laughed:

You can't be serious!
What you really want is to have a vacation adventure in Alexandria.
Forget about it; don't be silly—why waste your time?
Why leave Cairo to investigate something that may not even be a reality?

Their well-meaning taunts only urged me on.

Traveling to Siwa oasis in 1965 was time-consuming and difficult. I left Cairo Sunday, April 11th, on the morning train to Alexandria and then changed trains at Alex for the long, slow journey that would take me westward to Mersa Matruh, a sleepy port along the Mediterranean coast. Reaching Matruh station I learned that the weekly bus to Siwa was scheduled to leave at 5:00 AM the following morning. I spent the night at the local Youth Hostel where a number of German and Canadian hitchhikers were holding forth on the various transportation methods and unusual experiences while traveling across North Africa. Tired, I abandoned their conversation and went to bed. The manager woke me at 4:00 AM, prepared hot tea, and then directed me to the bus compound about a half mile to the southeast.

When I arrived the near-dark compound already was more than half filled with travelers, relatives, friends, and vendors. I checked with the ticket representative then mingled with the crowd. I found myself among many Siwans returning home to attend the *mulid*. The Siwan men were dressed in white robes that resembled Greek togas. They stayed apart from their women and children and talked quietly among themselves. The Siwan women, shrouded with dark indigo-dyed shawls embroidered with multi-colored geometric designs, sat quietly on the ground in isolated groups distant from their male relatives. Siwan girls wore multi-colored, flowered dresses, bedecked with amber-like, plastic necklaces and silver earrings. They formed groups and seemed to be satisfied as they played hand games using loops of string. Siwan boys were dressed simply in striped "nightshirt-style" *kuftans*. Each boy's head was shaved except for a residual tuft purposefully left so should an unforeseen calamity befall before his time, an angel could grasp this hand-hold and pull the child to heaven. Stashed among the milling group were piles of well-worn, tattered suitcases and satchels, crates of chickens, and four sheep. All ultimately would find their places aboard the bus.

What passed as a bus was parked in the middle of the compound. Most transportation companies would have retired this vehicle many decades earlier and would have blessed it for fine service. The ticket agent related to me that for almost twenty years after World War II drivers still coaxed its engine to complete the weekly 180 mile southward journey to the oasis. He explained with a smile how the axels rebounded, crunched and creaked over countless ruts as under-inflated patched tires strained to reach the Siwa. He wished me well and a safe journey.

The proscribed time for departure of 5:00 AM came and passed. About 5:45 voices in the compound stirred, a hopeful signal that the bus driver had arrived. Immediately there was a rush of people towards the bus. Our tickets were checked again as we pushed ourselves and our belongings through both front and rear access doors. Others climbed atop the bus and lashed baggage to the roof. Once aboard I found that all the window seats had been taken so I took an aisle seat on the left side. A Siwan man already seated in my row, tugged on my sleeve saying *ifadel* [please] and by doing so, offered me his window seat which I gladly accepted.

The ticket agent made his way one last time down the center aisle checking the number of passengers and ignoring the piles of baggage, animals in crates, and the four sheep. Satisfied that all was in order he departed. The driver then made a "grand entrance," gestured wildly, and in a loud voice welcomed everyone. He turned the key, the engine sputtered but started, and we were on our way. We experienced a smooth ride for the first two or three minutes then the paved road to Siwa ended on the southern outskirts of Mersa Matruh. After the first jolt of leaving the pavement we braced for a long jostling journey of bumps as we hit the first sequence of ruts that characterized the track southward into the desert.

The first hour passed . . . the ride was very uncomfortable. The oasis attracted our bus like a magnet as we were drawn further into the wasteland. The human spirit is tempered by such crossings and we were challenged by heat, dust, and thirst. By enduring such conditions weary desert travelers are bonded through sharing the same difficulties, the same problems, the same crises although the passengers reflect different ages, cultures, and nationalities.

Three hours into the journey . . . the monotony of the desert flat-land was interrupted. Off to the east a gazelle bounded in a loping gait and raced parallel to the bus. We weary travelers turned and gazed at the animal through dirt streaked windows packed and caked with fine dust particles. The gazelle ran slightly ahead of the bus, leaping and challenging the sleepy driver, conveying an unspoken message: accelerate, race me, and prove your human superiority.

The challenge raised was accepted. The driver turned sharply eastward and accelerated, leaving the rutted track. He gunned the engine and chased the gazelle across the flat, bumpy limestone plateau. The driver's decision to pursue the gazelle, however, was incautious since landmines remained in this region of the desert, relics of a past terrible war still hidden beneath the dusty earth just beyond the ill-defined border of safety. The bus driver ignored the potential dangers and continued eastward chasing the gazelle as it raced on ahead into the desert—too far, well beyond the ill-defined boundary where it would be madness to continue. The driver—to our relief and cheers—shouted *kefiya* [enough] and returned to the safety of the "road."

About five hours into the ride . . . the driver stopped so the passengers could relieve themselves. The men and boys exited, turned their back to the bus, and pissed while the women and girls shielded their eyes and remained aboard. About an hour later we stopped again, this time at a wooden tar paper and cardboard covered shack erected along the "road" where we could order tea and walk about to relieve our cramped legs. The women and girls left their seats but once outside, did not mingle with the males.

I attracted some attention as the only foreigner [*hawagah*] making the journey. To my surprise the Arabic spoken by most of the male travelers was modest and I could understand essentially their conversations and questions directed to me. This was because Arabic was not the primary language of these travelers; they spoke Siwi, an eastern dialect of the Berber language family, widely distributed across North Africa in more remote mountainous and oasis areas from Morocco eastward into Egypt.

> *Who are you?*
> *What is your country?*
> *Why are you going to al-Siwa?*
> *How is it that you can speak Arabic?*
> *How old are you?*
> *Are you married?*

I responded and asked them questions in return . . .

Time passed . . . we resumed our difficult journey southward across the desert . . .

I was lulled into a near hypnotic state where my mind and senses were dulled, so much so that I nearly missed the approach to the oasis. Suddenly without warning the desert tans and browns changed dramatically to reddish gold and violet hues. Throughout the bus the sleepy silence that characterized much of the journey was broken. A murmur arose, words spoken like a prayer, a single word repeated time and again burst from the parched lips of desert travelers, a word that meant more than a destination, a word that meant home and safety—*al-Siwa! al-Siwa! al-Siwa!*

The bus creaked and hurled down a narrow winding track cut into the edge of an eroded scarp—an enormous east-west trending cliff visible only during the last minutes of the trying journey. Like a slender keyhole the track pierced the north rim of the oasis and wound downward until it again straightened and stretched onward and southward more than 400 feet below the level of the sea. The valley floor beyond rushed forward as in a dream: the colors of sunset cast gold and red hues upon the land as I never before could have imagined. The emerald green of distant palms contrasted with the reddish earth; date palms filled with fruit stood outlined against the turquoise sky; the western horizon turned to gold as the afternoon sun emitted fiery bursts of glory.

My mind throbbed . . . the view westward revealed a mirage of fire, a shimmering vast salt lake that reflected dazzling spectrums of sunlight. Purple cliffs changed to dark blue and illuminated the eastern margins of the oasis where massive Mount Khamasia commanded the skyline, a rocky crag named after an obscure medieval Queen that once ruled this desert haven. Two mountains rose from the central floor of the valley standing as sentinels waiting to welcome weary travelers: the tallest resembled a honeycombed stone castle pierced by hundreds of hand-carved tombs, openings presenting silent puzzles to explorers who sought their mysterious origins. In the distance, multistoried houses reflected light as the setting sun struck the crystals of salt embedded in their stately walls.

Home at last to the Siwa: we had arrived!

What place is this, where the sun touches the tops of the western cliffs before the blue-black night ruled by the crescent horns of darkness shrouds the still valley? The Siwan passengers seized by emotion began a sing-song chant of homecoming. Tears filled the eyes of youthful and elderly desert warriors, running down dark shining faces and staining spotless robes of embroidered cotton and wool. Women raised their voices in ululations as their trilling added to the syncopation of the chanting. Home at last to the Siwa. The bus rang with laughter and thanksgiving: home at last to the Siwa!

I disembarked and encountered Hani al-Mogwadi, representative of the Egyptian government's civil service, posted to Siwa after his graduation from the University of Alexandria. He informed me that the *mulid* was scheduled to begin in three days on the evening of April 15th. I asked him whether or not it was permitted to document the ceremony on my tape recorder? He seemed amused by my question—why would anyone want to do so he asked me in return? I asked him again and he invited me into his office where he offered tea and prepared a hand-scribbled *tessreh* [permission] to be presented to the elders on the evening of the *mulid*. The document granted me permission to interview, photograph, and record the events. Hani apologized for the "problem" of accommodations [at this time there were no hotels at Siwa] and he arranged for me to stay at the modest government guest house located about a half mile south of the main town square. I was guided through Siwa town to the guest house by Tarik ibn al-Toumi who during the next several days answered my questions and prepared me for the events to come. I always will be grateful to Tarik for sharing with me the overall structure of the ceremony, how it would be organized, and how the events would unfold on the 15th.

Reflections on the *Mulid* (Festival)

On the evening of April 15th, 1965 I joined the residents of Siwa and nearby Qara oases and attended the *Mulid al-Kahana Thalthe* [Festival of the Third Priest]—an evening characterized by fire and drums, where chanting and rhythmic drumming excited and set our minds adrift. We assembled southeast of Siwa town beneath Aghourmi Mountain near *al-Taut es-Shamps* [the Sun's Well] where ancient ruined stones of rock salt—once part of the ancient oracle temple—towered above us. Waiting for the festivities to begin, we were offered dates, figs, and other oasis fruits presented in beautiful traditional Siwan baskets [*margunah*]. Our beverage that evening was *lubki*, prepared from fermented palm sap. Knowing the Muslim injunction towards intoxicating, fermented beverages, I asked two men seated on the ground next to me how it could be that *lubki* was permitted at the ceremony? They informed me with a smile that there was a tradition [*Hadith*] attributed to the Prophet, Mohammed, that allowed *lubki*-drinking since it was recorded that the Prophet had blessed the palm tree and had said: "All products of the date palm are permitted."

When the eating and drinking had ended we drew close and awaited the start of events. Presented here are sample passages reproduced from my field notes . . .

Five elders stood before us as the drumming increased in tempo and the fires cast their spitting embers skyward. The five walked slowly to a semi-circular place below the ruins of Aghourmi Mountain—a flat-topped outcrop—capped by the temple ruins. There, they took their seats of honor. We attending remained still in anticipation as tensions rose and flowed across the clearing. The evening cold was muted by an acacia brush and animal dung fire whose flames cast flickering shadows upon the smooth rock wall below the temple. Moonlight revealed the eager faces of hundreds seated on the dusty flat of cracked dried salt at the base of the rising mountain fortress.

The drumming crescendo increased in sound and tempo as gnarled hands continued their rhythmic pounding. The drumming resounded from cliffs ringing the valley. The tempo increased further: a blurred motion of hands striking the taunt dried skins of stinking sheep bladders stretched across elongate cylinders of clay. Rhythmic patterns darted across the darkness entering the spines of those assembled sending shivers of anticipation. The dung and brush desert fire flared and spit: sparks swirled skyward into the darkness of the star-studded sky.

All eyes rested upon the five elders who were dressed in robes of spun white wool, garments that resembled ancient Greek togas. The elders took their places at the edge of the flickering boundary of dark and light. The assembly grew still in anticipation, only the shrill cries and sounds of night-time birds and insects pierced the stillness.

The eldest elder stood and raised his hand slowly; he gazed at the crowd seated on the ground near him. He motioned to his right (to the north)—towards the largest of the signal drums: it was beaten once, then three times more. We were frozen in silence: no sound . . . and the chant began . . .

The eldest elder spoke first. When his verses were completed he returned to his chair as the second elder stood to take his turn. The chanted words enveloped the assembly. At the end of each verse the assembly repeated the last line in counterpoint as the elders pulsed and swayed to the rhythms of the drums. Time passed as the chant continued, the sounds rising and falling in intensity: rivulets of sweat flowed down the elders' faces. Reflected light from the full moon revealed the elders in more detail. Facial cuts and scars denoted their manhood initiation rites and tribal history. Two of the elders had foreheads marked by smallpox scars. As the chanting continued we slipped backward into history as the valley hummed with sounds of syncopated drumming . . . .

The Song of Siwa: Structure and Translation Issues

The saga linking the line of Marzuk with Iskander, The Third Priest, is recited in free verse by five elders who have as their sacred trust a hereditary duty to memorize the words. The epic represents an interesting amalgamation in that the primary language, Siwi, is interspersed regularly with identifiable Arabic loan words, and terms that appear to be representative of an ancient Proto-Berber language. The eldest elder is honored with the responsibility of reciting the most ancient portion of the chant. These initial verses are presented in groups of five un-rhymed lines, each spoken with a rhythm of fifteen counts. Once the fifth line of each group has been spoken, the assembly shouts out and repeats the last rhythmic seven counts, as with the following example:

Original:

15 counts:	*T'k ta-a-lat shampe tilit s'at manzu gunid bard,*
15 counts:	*Magro m'an Chemi balad min al-ramla bahr nahr,*
15 counts:	*Shukre attaf Siwa wadi, m'a taut weh myeh zeel,*
15 counts:	*Rakla dzeef ferzu dahab, nuvel min al-lil el-fa'dah,*
15 counts:	*Min leh nass em-tel al-Siwa, de ebla al ghan artf.*
7 counts:	**Za'qikla:** *De ebla al ghan artf.*

Translation:

15 counts:	Back three million fiery dawns when time was young and distant cold,
15 counts:	Westward from the land of Chemi past the sandy sea of fire,
15 counts:	Lay the hidden valley Siwa filled with *tauts* of water cool,

15 counts:	Ringed by cliffs of golden bronze that changed to silver with the night,
15 counts:	No one walked inside the Siwa, this before the time of man.
7 counts:	**Assembly:** This before the time of man.

Upon completion of these oldest verses the first elder gives way to the second and retires to his chair. The second elder resumes the chant but implements an alternative verse pattern that sets a different rhythm standard that thereafter is continued throughout delivery. In contrast to the first, this pattern is chanted in groups of four un-rhymed lines. Even these patterns and rhythms, however, are not consistent. Commonly, the first three lines are spoken with an eight count rhythm with a fourth line of seven or eight counts. The patterns, however, are variable in count, for example 8-8-8-8, 8-7-8-8, 8-7-7-8, 8-8-7-7, while a minority of verses may include 9 count rhythms. In all instances the last line is repeated and shouted out by those assembled as with the following examples:

Original and Translation:

8 counts:	*Ela jhma zu-rru bekhet,*
8 counts:	*Ghor-met, kal-met, sur'al ess'i,*
8 counts:	*Dhat me' marnuh fi al-dznel,*
8 counts:	*Ab'yd maleh fik Aghourmi.*
8 counts:	*Za'qikla: Ab'yd maleh fik Aghourmi.*

8 counts:	God descended—raced upon them,
8 counts:	Spinning, turning, joyful motion,
8 counts:	Lower 'till he landed on the,
8 counts:	Salt white walls above *Aghourmi.*
8 counts:	**Assembly:** Salt white walls above *Aghourmi.*

Original and Translation:

8 counts:	*El-mt etnin selt min om'ha,*
7 counts:	*Wah'd lazmebes a-hamut,*
7 counts:	*'Qu-nun bela 'qu-nun beh,*
8 counts:	*Bes al-wahid iste huk-kam.*
8 counts:	*Za'qikla: Bes al-wahid iste huk-kam.*

8 counts:	When two are birthed at mother's time,
7 counts:	One must for the other die,
7 counts:	Law of tribe and law of beast,
8 counts:	Proclaim that only one can rule.
8 counts:	**Assembly:** Proclaim that only one can rule.

Original and Translation:

8 counts:	*Mzka'lm der-re Zo-ser,*
8 counts:	*Uqa' Hagzer—makzr Temsl,*
7 counts:	*Mala saghura sokkneh,*
7 counts:	*Sekhmet ardsh' ha-minah.*
7 counts:	***Za'qikla:*** *Sekhmet ardsh' ha-minah.*

8 counts:	Past the court of once proud Zo-ser,
8 counts:	Fallen ruins—broken statues,
7 counts:	Goddess of the desert heat,
7 counts:	Sekhmet guided healing priests.
7 counts:	**Assembly:** Sekhmet guided healing priests.

Each elder upon completion of his component gives way to the next in line. This alternating pattern is repeated throughout the evening until the eldest elder rises to recite the final and shortest passages. These last verses bring the *mulid's* activities to a point of highest anticipation as the words are said to conjure and reconfirm the return of Iskander's spirit to the Siwa.

Upon the conclusion of the chant a cluster of events follow that culminat with the unveiling of the relic—the highlight of the evening—an object with both religious and historical meaning for all Siwans. Description of the events associated with the unveiling of the relic—as recorded in my field notes—follow my translation of the epic . . .

PART 2

Presentation and Translation:
The Song of Siwa

The First Elder rises and recites . . . [Lines 1-65].

Ebte'da

1. *T'k ta-a-lat shampe tilit, s'at manzu gunid bard*
2. *Magro m'an Chemi balad, min al-ramla bahr nahr*
3. *Shukre attaf Siwa wadi, m'a taut weh myeh zeel*
4. *Rakla dzeef ferzu dahab, nuvel min al-lil ef-fadah*
5. *Min leh nass em-tel al-Siwa, de ebla al ghan artf.*
   Za'qikla: *De ebla al ghan artf.*

Beginning

1. Back three million fiery dawns, when time was young and distant cold,
2. Westward from the land of Chem, past the sandy sea of fire,
3. Lay the hidden valley Siwa, filled with *tauts* of water cool.
4. Ringed by cliffs of golden bronze, that changed to silver with the night,
5. No one walked inside the Siwa, this before the time of man.
   Assembly: This before the time of man.

6. Back three million fiery dawns, near the sea once called the *Vanton,*
7. Hunters lived in caves of stone, inside the mountains safe from beasts.
8. Ice was grinding slowly southward, bringing cold and chilling rain.
9. Hunters dressed in skins and masks, painted symbols in their caverns,
10. Signs of magic brushed with blood, chanting for the gods' protection.
    Assembly: Chanting for the gods' protection.

11. Hunters gathered left their mountains, trekked on southward towards the sea.

12. Marzuk led the clan of hunters, down steep valleys towards the shore.

13. Camping near the graceful pines, that lined the seaside cliffs of stone,

14. Fresh the southern salty air, co-mingled with the scent of god.

15. Through the gentle bending pines, came a night time dream of vision . . .

    Assembly: Came a night time dream of vision . . .

16. Tall the pine trees bent and murmured, spoke as one their whispered words:

17. *Marzuk heed us ice is coming, spoke the voices through the pines,*

18. *Cut our bodies take us gladly, use your axes made of stone.*

19. *Build ten rafts upon the shoreline, build ten rafts and save your clan,*

20. *Flee you Marzuk cross the Vanton, save your people from the ice.*

    Assembly: Save your people from the ice.

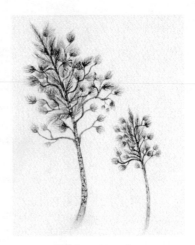

Whispering pines

21. Marzuk puzzled by his vision, shared his dream with all the clan.

22. Some believed but others murmured, danger lay within such words . . .

23. *Hunters who are strong and able, must not sail upon the sea.*

24. *Death awaits us on the waters, thrashing beasts will claim our lives,*

25. *We are safe upon the land, the Vanton offers only death.*

    Assembly: The Vanton offers only death.

26. Marzuk in the days that followed, walked alone among the pines.
27. Marzuk felled the stately trees, who cried out to him *save the clan.*
28. Marzuk tied the timbers tight, with slender strips of skin from beasts.
29. Marzuk pitched and sealed the rafts, then from the central spars he lashed,
30. Sails of woven hides to catch, the breath of god his friend the wind.

    Assembly: The breath of god his friend the wind.

31. Came a time the rafts completed, Marzuk called the clan to meet.
32. Some rejected would not follow, claimed his dreams were evil signs,
33. Sent by spirits from the past, who would harm the clan of hunters.
34. Others placed their faith in Marzuk's, dreams of safety from the cold,
35. They would join and follow Marzuk, sail across the dark black sea.

    Assembly: Sail across the dark black sea.

Marzuk, leader of the clan

36. When the sun had risen twice, each declared their choice for action.
37. Down the winding seaward path, bearded hunters led their women,
38. Chanting words from ancient times, voices asked for god's protection.
39. Out upon the strand they stepped, as gentle winds and pines grew still,
40. Cold the waters lapped about them, clansmen, friends were left behind.

    Assembly: Clansmen, friends were left behind.

41. Strong the winds blew ever southward, faint and distant lost from sight.

42. White-topped waves alive with foam, streaked the beards of fur-clad hunters.

43. Gentle days gave way to storms, dark cold waves attacked their bodies,

44. Lifted rafts and frightened men, downward pulled the rushing waters,

45. Crashing on the wave-tossed pine rafts, pitched and hurled them through the sea.
    Assembly: Pitched and hurled them through the sea.

46. Seven days with equal nights, the storm its southward course would hold,

47. Sickness fear of death by sea, hunters chanted—*Marzuk save us.*

48. All about them howling winds, crashing waves proclaimed the danger.

49. Some grew weak and lost their courage, water fingers touched their legs,

50. Grasped and pulled them from the others, lost forever in the sea.
    Assembly: Lost forever in the sea.

Crossing the Sea of Vanton

51. Seven days with equal nights, clansmen sailed upon the *Vanton.*

52. But came a dawn of morning light, as the sun broke through the clouds,

53. Winds blew soft the sea grew calm, Marzuk shouted in the distance,

54. High were rising bluish mountains, wooded peaks inside the clouds,

Reaching the southern shore

55. Gently resting on the shore, rafts lay still their journey ended.
    Assembly: Rafts lay still their journey ended.

56. In the distant northern land, that lined the seaside cliffs and caves,

57. Near the tall and graceful pines, that watched in silence quiet still,

58. Screams and cries from those who doubted, *grant us time to make our rafts.*

59. Down the mountain slopes there poured, a moving grinding mass of death.

60. Trapped by ice they spoke no more, they had rejected god's own word.
    Assembly: They had rejected god's own word.

61. Back three million fiery dawns, the clan of Marzuk left their home.

62. God had saved them given strength, to live again each day with hope.

63. Westward from the endless river, distant from the land of Chem,

64. Ringed by cliffs of golden bronze, that changed to silver with the night,

65. Lay the hidden valley Siwa, waiting for the breath of man.
    Assembly: Waiting for the breath of man.

The Second Elder rises and recites . . . [Lines 66-149].

Etmas'sh shar-ke

66. *Th'n mas-qa-ma erd gid-didah,*
67. *Zol ed-diml a'la nas-sh,*
68. *Lazum a'mal tasm-in sabin*
69. *Lazum ik-sr ga-did i-yhel.*
    Za'qikla: *Lazum ik-sr ga-did i-yhel.*

Eastward

66. Yet the hardships of the new land,
67. Ever pressed upon the clansmen,
68. Forced them make a harsh decision,
69. Forced them break their new formed roots.
    Assembly: Forced them break their new formed roots.

70. From this schism one such section,
71. Traveled southward then turned eastward,
72. Through tall mountains capped with ice,
73. Onward marched the clan of Marzuk.
    Assembly: Onward marched the clan of Marzuk.

74. Marzuk he the able hunter,
75. Marzuk he with strength of many,
76. Marzuk who could make new fire,
77. Chosen by the clan to lead.
    Assembly: Chosen by the clan to lead.

78. Stronger men helped weaker others,
79. For the march was slow and painful,
80. Elders carried youngest children,
81. Onward marched the clan of Marzuk.
      Assembly: Onward marched the clan of Marzuk.

82. Danger tracked them like *razallah*,
83. Some grew weary ever doubtful,
84. Water illness stalked them daily,
85. Many died with spotted sickness.
      Assembly: Many died with spotted sickness.

86. Shamans could not heal their bodies,
87. Graves were marked by purple stones,
88. Bones of vision cast by shamans,
89. Told no reason why men died.
      Assembly: Told no reason why men died.

90. Marzuk took the elder's council,
91. Led them southward through the mountains,
92. Far from danger ever lurking,
93. Leaving sickness by the sea.
      Assembly: Leaving sickness by the sea.

94. Yet the tree-lined mountain passage,
95. Drew them to an endless desert,
96. Where the high and drifting sand dunes,
97. Rose and towered o'er the clan.
      Assembly: Rose and towered o'er the clan.

98. In this place of desolation,
99. People cried: *he has betrayed us,*
100. In this place of endless sand dunes,
101. People cried out: *we are lost!*
      Assembly: People cried out: we are lost!

102. In the turquoise upper heaven,
103. High above their downcast faces,
104. Flashed a star that glowed in daytime,
105. Then downward from the home of god—
    Assembly: Then downward from the home of god—

106. Appeared a bird with brilliant feathers,
107. Downward circled and descended,
108. Landing on the staff of Marzuk,
109. All the people saw the sign.
    Assembly: All the people saw the sign.

Messenger bird from god Zagilie

110. Messenger from god *Zagilie*,
111. God-sent bird with shining feathers,
112. God's bird not seen on earth before,
113. Led them to a hidden spring.
    Assembly: Led them to a hidden spring.

114. Cool the flow of sparkling waters,
115. Out from the *taut* of mother earth,
116. Gave new hope for their salvation,
117. Hope and joy from god *Zagilie*.
    Assembly: Hope and joy from god *Zagilie*.

118. Marzuk's mate the dark-haired Gosla,
119. She the strongest of the women,
120. Gosla daughter of Etomie,
121. Made a promise to *Zagilie*:
    Assembly: Made a promise to *Zagilie*:

Gosla, mate of Marzuk

122. *If you the bird of god will linger,*
123. *Help us find a peaceful haven,*
124. *Tauts where waters gush with sweetness,*
125. *Where the hunted beasts are plenty—*
     Assembly: Where the hunted beasts are plenty—

126. *I will build a sacred temple,*
127. *One of grandeur and devotion,*
128. *And forever time to come our,*
129. *Hearts will honor god Zagilie.*
     Assembly: Hearts will honor god *Zagilie.*

130. With her words god's bird flew skyward,
131. Soaring high above the desert,
132. Higher, rising towards the heavens,
133. Twisting, turning out of sight.
     Assembly: Twisting, turning out of sight.

134. Thala aged wrinkled mother,
135. Yet whose eyesight was the keenest,
136. Saw the object floating downward,
137. Multicolored and reflecting—
     Assembly: Multicolored and reflecting—

138. A colored feather downward drifted,
139. Landed at the feet of Marzuk,
140. *Zagilie's sign*—the people shouted,
141. God protect us we are saved.
     Assembly: God protect us we are saved.

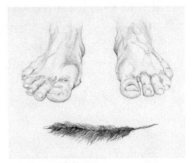

Messenger bird's sacred feather

40

142. *Marzuk lead us—cried the clansmen,*
143. *Marzuk lead us—women shouted,*
144. *Take us to the hidden valley,*
145. *Where our home at last will be.*
    Assembly: Where our home at last will be.

146. Eyes of Gosla wet with teardrops,
147. Sought her husband and together,
148. Marching eastward led the tribesmen,
149. Onward towards the rising sun.
    Assembly: Onward towards the rising sun.

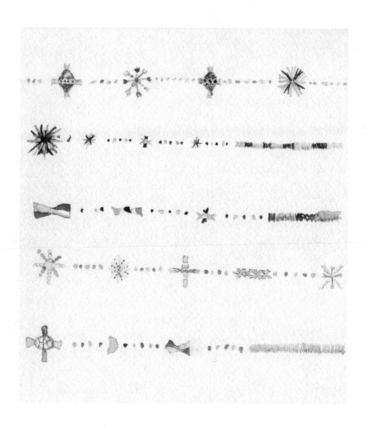

The Third Elder rises and recites . . . [Lines 150-277]

Wu'ud

150. *Shamps sabbah we tallat-tin-e,*
151. *Ma-fsh amman fil ak-mas-fah,*
152. *Nas-sme muh-if ma'at gham-bi,*
153. *Rab-ebbal wa'id ru'yah.*
    Za'qikla: *Rab-ebbal wa'id ru'yah.*

Promise

150. Seven suns then thirty more but,
151. Still no haven in the distance,
152. Many feared that death was certain,
153. God-sent promise just a vision.
    Assembly: God-sent promise just a vision.

154. Devh the bearded son of Taleg,
155. Ran ahead and climbed a sand dune,
156. From the crest he saw more desert,
157. Yet the wasteland scene was changing—
    Assembly: Yet the wasteland scene was changing—

158. With the aid of dusk's warm shadows,
159. Devh saw the desert floor transformed,
160. Through rippling bands of desert heat,
161. First a vision then more clearly—
    Assembly: First a vision then more clearly—

162. There—an onward stretching valley,
163. Ribbed by cliffs reflecting sunlight,
164. Where ten thousand suns were dancing,
165. Wildly twisting never stopping.
    Assembly: Wildly twisting never stopping.

166. Green the color of the valley,
167. Shades of gold and tints of silver,
168. As the vision spread before them,
169. Eastward marched the clan of Marzuk.
    Assembly: Eastward marched the clan of Marzuk.

170. Voices raised that echoed glory,
171. All praise for god's protective hand,
172. Here was land where all could flourish,
173. Home at last where all could see—
    Assembly: Home at last where all could see—

174. Giant herds of black-striped *zelda,*
175. Giant herds of meat-beast *vedro*;
176. Many *tauts* with waters flowing,
177. Food and drink for all the clan.
    Assembly: Food and drink for all the clan.

178. In the center of the valley,
179. Rose a mountain jutting skyward,
180. Like a slender tribal watchman,
181. Standing guard o'er all the clan.
    Assembly: Standing guard o'er all the clan.

182. Upon this hill they named *Aghourmi,*
183. Gosla built *Zagilie's* temple,
184. All took part with thankful hands,
185. They built a home to honor god.
    Assembly: They built a home to honor god.

186. Day by day the people labored,
187. Each rock-salt stone was set by hand,
188. Marzuk called the clan to gather,
189. Each brought treasure for the god.
    Assembly: Each brought treasure for the god.

190. Sacred stones that fell from heaven,
191. Green stones like the eyes of *belda,*
192. Stones with shells of yellow color,
193. Rich the god's own treasure grew.
    Assembly: Rich the god's own treasure grew.

194. O'er the valley sounds were muted,
195. As when evening time approaches,
196. The sunset sky soon filled with birds,
197. Singing praise to god *Zagilie.*
    Assembly: Singing praise to god *Zagilie.*

198. From the highest northern heaven,
199. Bursting forth with sudden glory,
200. Casting flames with fiery tracings,
201. O'er the boundless sky above—
    Assembly: O'er the boundless sky above—

202. God descend—raced upon them,
203. Spinning, turning, joyful motion,
204. Lower 'till he rested on the,
205. Salt white walls above *Aghourmi.*
    Assembly: Salt white walls above *Aghourmi.*

206. All the earth stood quiet, waiting,
207. Birds grew silent heartbeats quickened,
208. People fell upon the earth,
209. Dared not look upon god's face.
    Assembly: Dared not look upon god's face.

210. Spoken words from god *Zagilie*,
211. Spoken to the clan of Marzuk,
212. Words that filled their hearts with joy,
213. *Zagilie* made his wishes known:
    Assembly: *Zagilie* made his wishes known:

214. *Your journey hard is now complete,*
215. *Here the Siwa greets you gladly,*
216. *Use the waters, fruits, and meat-beasts,*
217. *You will find a life that pleases.*
    Assembly: You will find a life that pleases.

218. *I, Zagilie, will protect you,*
219. *Keep you well and safe from harm,*
220. *I, Zagilie, will protect you,*
221. *But you must follow what I say:*
    Assembly: But you must follow what I say:

222. *Mothers who would ever serve me—*
223. *Sew upon your dress of black,*
224. *Signs of sunburst like my feathers,*
225. *I Zagilie am your god.*
    Assembly: I *Zagilie* am your god.

226. *Fathers who would ever serve me—*
227. *For your eldest daughters make,*
228. *Disks from finest mountain silver,*
229. *I Zagilie am your god.*
    Assembly: I *Zagilie* am your god.

230. *Daughters who would ever serve me—*
231. *Wear your discs of polished silver,*
232. *Waking hours, morning, evening,*
233. *I Zagilie am your god.*
    Assembly: I Zagilie am your god.

Unmarried girl's virginity disk

234. *When husbands take you for their brides,*
235. *Pass your discs to younger sisters,*
236. *Join together wife and husband—*
237. *I Zagilie am your god.*
   Assembly: I *Zagilie* am your god.

238. *Young sons who would ever serve me—*
239. *Follow in the ways of Marzuk,*
240. *Honor both your fathers, mothers*
241. *I Zagilie am your god.*
   Assembly: I *Zagilie* am your god.

242. *Faithful Gosla stand before me,*
243. *Mate of Marzuk stand before me,*
244. *For all time your line will flourish,*
245. *Strong and just will be your son—*
   Assembly: Strong and just will be your son—

246. *A King to lead within the Siwa,*
247. *Wise to hear his elder's council,*
248. *Truthful he will serve all people,*
249. *Share with each the ways of god.*
   Assembly: Share with each the ways of god.

250. *Symbolic of his high position,*
251. *He will wear the horns of Gurzel,*
252. *He will reign till oldness takes him.*
253. *Then his son will wear the horns.*
   Assembly: Then his son will wear the horns.

254. *Clan of Marzuk keep my symbols,*
255. *Ever tend my temple flame,*
256. *You will lead good lives abundant,*
257. *Free from conquest, war and death.*
   Assembly: Free from conquest, war and death.

258. *Zagilie's* hand then blocked the sun,
259. As noon-time darkness fell upon them—
260. *Clan of Marzuk heed my wishes—*
261. *Ever tend my temple flame.*
    Assembly: Ever tend my temple flame.

God Zagilie blocks the sun

262. Then rose voices from the children,
263. Words of god's protecting glory,
264. Sounds that echoed from the mountains,
265. Past the lake whose depths are endless—
    Assembly: Past the lake whose depths are endless—

266. Children's voices—rising higher,
267. *Zagilie Si-wa*—you we honor,
268. Sounds that echoed 'cross the valley,
269. *Si-wa! Si-wa! Si-wa! Si-wa!*
    Assembly: Si-wa! Si-wa! Si-wa! Si-wa!

270. *Zagilie's* hand returned the sun,
271. The disk of darkness was removed,
272. The earth now warmed by gentle light,
273. As god's sunshine blessed them all.
    Assembly: As god's sunshine blessed them all.

274. *Zagilie's* rock-salt temple walls,
275. Reflected bright the noon-time sun,
276. Sent their eyes ablaze with visions,
277. God *Zagilie* dwelt among them.
    Assembly: God *Zagilie* dwelt among them.

The Fourth Elder rises and recites . . . [Lines 278-489].

Bul'ugh

278. *Nep-td estad et'bah Hai-win,*
279. *Shil-me rim-aah darf al-sulfah,*
280. *Hadd al-rum'ah dz-mal har-f,*
281. *Mi-daz far'van 'trg-nah ha'daf.*
    Za'qikla: *Mi-daz far'van 'trg-nah ha'daf.*

Manhood

278. Start the hunt and track the meat beasts,
279. Bring your spears each tipped with flint,
280. Keen their sharpened scalloped edges,
281. Straight and true will find their mark.
    Assembly: Straight and true will find their mark.

282. Track and stalk the clever meat beasts,
283. He with stealth and careful patience,
284. He with keenest observation,
285. He shall gain the meat beast prize.
    Assembly: He shall gain the meat beast prize.

286. Trace your hand upon the damp ground,
287. Tracks of *farna* tracks of *belda,*
288. See the pattern of their footsteps,
289. See the marks of sliding tail.
    Assembly: See the marks of sliding tail.

290. The *farna* walked just moments past,
291. See the edges of his tracks,
292. Sharp and clean upon the sand,
293. Wind has not yet blurred their mark.
    Assembly: Wind has not yet blurred their mark.

294. The *farna* paces, seeks his prey,
295. The *farna's* skin most highly prized,
296. For the honor that men gain by,
297. Disregarding hunting danger.
    Assembly: Disregarding hunting danger.

298. Marzuk King of Siwa Valley,
299. Sought each beast of prey in season,
300. Marzuk wore about his neck,
301. Eighteen fangs from hunting valor.
    Assembly: Eighteen fangs from hunting valor.

302. Marzuk conquered nine such *farna*,
303. Who left their claw-marks on his chest,
304. Scars of courage from the hunting,
305. He was bravest, he was King.
    Assembly: He was bravest, he was King.

306. Seasons passed and then more seasons,
307. Gosla felt within her body,
308. First a movement then a stirring,
309. Life was growing day by day.
    Assembly: Life was growing day by day.

310. When the moon grew full and yellow,
311. Gosla came to woman's firmness,
312. Felt the first pains of the birthing,
313. Gosla cried—*my time has come.*
    Assembly: Gosla cried—*my time has come.*

314. Women walked her through the evening,
315. Three times 'round *Aghourmi* Mountain,
316. Chanting for the god to aid her:
317. *God Zagilie ease her birth.*
   Assembly: God Zagilie ease her birth.

318. The hearth of Glim their destination,
319. She the wizened birthing woman,
320. Glim knew which herbs would ease the pain,
321. Learned from Ard in ages past.
   Assembly: Learned from Ard in ages past.

322. Glim the wizened birthing woman,
323. Held the right hand of Queen Gosla,
324. Felt the motions in her belly,
325. Chanted words from ancient times—
   Assembly: Chanted words from ancient times—

326. *Gosla—shick rr-urie abni,*
327. Gosla—a son you soon will bear,
328. *Gosla—oma regna tagzult,*
329. Gosla—mother of a King!
   Assembly: Gosla—mother of a King!

330. Glim prepared the drink of birthing,
331. The bitter taste would dull the pain,
332. Gosla labored through the chanting,
333. Soon the time of birth would come.
   Assembly: Soon the time of birth would come.

334. Gosla rode the stool of birthing,
335. Glim and Gosla spoke the magic—
336. *Tzk amtu slo dek naah barring,*
337. Words to ward off night-time spirits.
   Assembly: Words to ward off night-time spirits.

338.   But at this time of Gosla's birthing,
339.   Came not one son—but two in likeness,
340.   Shrill the shouts screamed out by Glim,
341.   Those attending felt the fear.
       Assembly: Those attending felt the fear.

342.   Through the blood red mists of birthing,
343.   Gosla screamed—*I am the Queen,*
344.   By her words she stayed the knife,
345.   That would have slayed one of her twins.
       Assembly: That would have slayed one of her twins.

346.   No one heeded spoken warnings,
347.   From that distant night of pain,
348.   *When two are birthed at mother's time,*
349.   *One must for the other die.*
       Assembly: One must for the other die.

350.   Through the years both grew and prospered,
351.   Zel and Zechen twins of Gosla,
352.   Both honored family and the clan,
353.   Father-mother gave each love.
       Assembly: Father-mother gave each love.

354.   Through the years both grew and prospered,
355.   Zel and Zechen twins of Marzuk,
356.   Beardless cheeks gave way to manhood,
357.   Both the sons had grown to men.
       Assembly: Both the sons had grown to men.

358.   Came the time, their test of manhood,
359.   That the laws of clan required,
360.   Each must prove their strength and courage,
361.   Each must prove their hunting valor.
       Assembly: Each must prove their hunting valor.

362. First each son must bear the cuttings,
363. Before each youth could be called man,
364. Rites of manhood culled the weakest,
365. Only strongest could survive.
    Assembly: Only strongest could survive.

366. Sit inside the ring of hunters,
367. Next to father—next to elder,
368. Next to men—who led the clan,
369. Next to father, King, and elder.
    Assembly: Next to father, King, and elder.

370. Day drumming—night of fire,
371. Announced to all the rite of passage,
372. Zel and Zechen stripped their garments,
373. Stood before the men's assembly.
    Assembly: Stood before the men's assembly.

374. Fighting back the doubts of youth,
375. Standing tall before the elders,
376. Crackling fire and pounding drumming,
377. Rhythms from the dawn of time.
    Assembly: Rhythms from the dawn of time.

378. Both stood quiet without motion,
379. Fighting off the cold of night,
380. Fear of failure gave each strength to,
381. Face the fearful dancing demons.
    Assembly: Face the fearful dancing demons.

382. Once the rhythmic chanting ended,
383. Slowly both were beckoned forward,
384. Zel and Zechen faced the elders,
385. Wearing painted masks of *khell*.
    Assembly: Wearing painted masks of *khell*.

386. Sweat drenched hands of dancing elders,
387. Held the cutting knives of manhood,
388. Light reflected from the blades that,
389. Flashed the pain the knives would bring.
    Assembly: Flashed the pain the knives would bring.

390. Zel and Zechen sons of Marzuk,
391. Bore the cuts and lost their youth,
392. Blood flowed down across their bodies,
393. Transforming each from youth to man.
    Assembly: Transforming each from youth to man.

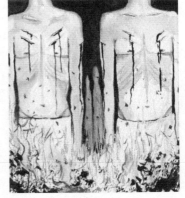

Clan manhood scarification rites

394. From the darkness of the shadows,
395. Danced the spirits dressed in masks,
396. Standing elders chanting louder,
397. Blood of manhood boiling higher—
    Assembly: Blood of manhood boiling higher—

398. One by one each took their places,
399. Formed the sacred chain of men,
400. Now the sons of Marzuk danced,
401. Ever closer—voices screaming—
    Assembly: Ever closer—voices screaming—

402. Zel and Zechen shared the movements,
403. Faster-faster-ever faster,
404. Till the seed of manhood left them,
405. Spilling onto mother earth.
    Assembly: Spilling onto mother earth.

406. Ashes from the ritual fire,
407. Crushed together with a *teglast*,
408. Mixed with earth and seed from man,
409. Smeared upon their bleeding bodies.
    Assembly: Smeared upon their bleeding bodies.

410. Zel and Zechen fought the blackness,
411. Bore the pain without emotion,
412. Standing near the blazing fire,
413. Each had passed from youth to man.
    Assembly: Each had passed from youth to man.

414. Praise and honor to their father,
415. Each had born the cuts in silence,
416. Praise and honor to their mother,
417. Now each rested, gathered strength.
    Assembly: Now each rested gathered strength.

418. Three dawns later twins of Marzuk,
419. Stood before the tribal elders,
420. Now as men but still not hunters,
421. Next the trials of fast and hunting.
    Assembly: Next the trials of fast and hunting.

422. No food allowed for seven days,
423. Only water from the *taut,*
424. Time to cleanse their body temple,
425. Time to seek the proper spirit.
    Assembly: Time to seek the proper spirit.

426. On the morning of the seventh,
427. Came the test of hunting skill,
428. Each was given two flint stones,
429. With antler horn they flaked their blades.
    Assembly: With antler horn they flaked their blades.

Zel's spear blade

55

430. Using skills taught by their father,
431. Each must stalk and kill a *farna*,
432. Cut out its heart, cut off its claws,
433. Proof that they were able hunters.
    Assembly: Proof that they were able hunters.

434. Seven dawns of fast plus two,
435. Daylight found the brothers hungry,
436. Muscles tensed their bodies gleaming,
437. From the balms each had applied.
    Assembly: From the balms each had applied.

438. Would they pass their tests as hunters?
439. Would they fail, return in shame?
440. Each twin clasped his brother's hand,
441. No words spoken—turned and parted.
    Assembly: No words spoken—turned and parted.

442. Zechen he would travel northward,
443. Where *farna's* den he knew would,
444. Be among the fallen stones that,
445. Formed the rocky northern scarp.
    Assembly: Formed the rocky northern scarp.

446. Zel would choose a different track,
447. He traveled southward towards the *taut*,
448. Where he knew the spotted *farna*,
449. Could be careless as it drank.
    Assembly: Could be careless as it drank.

450. Neither knew upon their parting,
451. They never more again would meet,
452. Zel and Zechen twins of Marzuk,
453. One would live—the other die.
    Assembly: One would live—the other die.

454. Climbing down the rocky scarp,
455. Zechen fell and snapped his spear blade,
456. As he knelt to make another,
457. Footsteps bringing death approached.
    Assembly: Footsteps bringing death approached.

458. Zechen son of Marzuk—Gosla,
459. Turned and faced the striped *farna*,
460. Only briefly saw its leap,
461. Heard the snarling beast descend.
    Assembly: Heard the snarling beast descend.

462. Southward near the *taut* of *zeitun*,
463. Crouched in hiding Zel was waiting,
464. Though his hunger grew impatient,
465. Though his thirst a raging torment.
    Assembly: Though his thirst a raging torment.

466. Slinking towards the cooling waters,
467. Came the *farna* softly stepping,
468. Came the *farna's* padded footsteps,
469. The careless *farna* paused to drink.
    Assembly: The careless *farna* paused to drink.

470. Zel leaped out in savage fury,
471. *Farna* claws slashed o'er his body,
472. Twice he plunged his knife and twisted,
473. Heard the *farna's* blood-choked screams.
    Assembly: Heard the *farna's* blood-choked screams.

474. Waters from the *taut* of *zeitun*,
475. Soothed his deep-torn hunting wounds,
476. Zel with haste would skin the *farna*,
477. Using skills he gained from father.
    Assembly: Using skills he gained from father.

478. Zel raised his knife of manly hunter,
479. Slit through sinew, muscle, tissue,
480. Touched the beast's still beating heart,
481. Gleaming like a throbbing sun.
     Assembly: Gleaming like a throbbing sun.

482. He had passed the test of manhood—
483. He had passed the test of hunger—
484. He had passed the test of thirst—
485. He had passed the test of hunting.
     Assembly: He had passed the test of hunting.

486. Zel ripped the heart out from the *farna*,
487. Zel the hunter held it high—
488. Shouted loud across the valley—
489. *Father—I have honored thee!*
     Assembly: Father—I have honored thee!

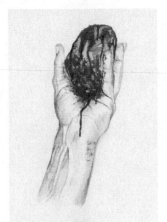

Holding the farna's still beating heart

The Fifth Elder rises and recites . . . [Lines 490-573].

Mah-ht

490. *'Etnein ed'rab sa'ab en-fas-iel*
491. *Wa-gah Marzuk baq'e di-man,*
492. *Heba maz-tum ibno Zechen,*
493. *Sa'id maha-ra mas-ta'lim.*
     Za'qikla: *Sa'id maha-ra mas-ta'lim.*

Death

490. Two times seven seasons passed,
491. But did not soften Marzuk's pain,
492. Had he failed his dead son Zechen,
493. Not taught skills of proper hunting?
     Assembly: Not taught skills of proper hunting?

494. Fate had willed to Zechen death,
495. Still the words of midwife Glim,
496. Sounded on the night of birth,
497. Rang ever clear within his mind:
     Assembly: Rang ever clear within his mind:

498. *When two are birthed at mother's time,*
499. *One must for the other die,*
500. *Law of tribe and law of beast,*
501. *Proclaim that only one can rule.*
     Assembly: Proclaim that only one can rule.

502. Could the twins have shared the crown?
503. Or would hate and bitter actions,
504. Tear through family line and cause the,
505. Self-destruction of the clan?
    Assembly: Self-destruction of the clan?

506. Seasons passed and then more seasons,
507. Giving change to King and Queen.
508. Marzuk's hair had turned to grey,
509. Gosla walked with curved-arched back.
    Assembly: Gosla walked with curved-arched back.

510. Yet her eyes still spoke at night,
511. Eyes that recalled happy moments,
512. When both had climbed the hill of love,
513. That changed into quick rising mountains—
    Assembly: That changed into quick rising mountains—

514. Until at last both reached the top,
515. Where heavens glory burst upon them,
516. Leaving both to drift together,
517. Falling gently to the earth.
    Assembly: Falling gently to the earth.

518. God had given lives of joy where,
519. Love had grown with passing seasons,
520. Lives that echoed love and passion,
521. Filled with care and happiness.
    Assembly: Filled with care and happiness.

522. Came the day cold swirled about her,
523. Came the day Queen Gosla faltered,
524. Death was stalking Gosla's spirit,
525. Still she fought with fierce abandon.
    Assembly: Still she fought with fierce abandon.

526. Marzuk, Zel, and others gathered,
527. Pale and ashen lay the Queen,
528. Clouded eyes fixed on her mate,
529. Eyes that spoke true words of love.
    Assembly: Eyes that spoke true words of love.

530. Came the moment Marzuk dreaded,
531. Came the time her spirit flew—
532. Rose and merged with god *Zagilie*,
533. No more to walk upon the earth.
    Assembly: No more to walk upon the earth.

534. All the clan stood hushed in silence,
535. Winds of sadness blew upon them,
536. Death's dry dust swirled all about them,
537. Each family's hearth lay cold in mourning.
    Assembly: Each family's hearth lay cold in mourning.

538. Clansmen knelt and offered honor,
539. Marzuk wrapped his mate in furs,
540. Placed blue stones around her neck,
541. Symbols of her clan and station.
    Assembly: Symbols of her clan and station.

542. Slowly stepping towards the *Mouta*,
543. Hill of *Mouta*—place of spirits,
544. Clansmen stepping towards the *Mouta*,
545. Place of bones and home of death.
    Assembly: Place of bones and home of death.

Gosla's funeral procession

546. Marzuk bore the Queen in silence,
547. Wailing sobs of anguished women,
548. Silent tears of brave young warriors,
549. Marked the path to open grave.
   Assembly: Marked the path to open grave.

550. Now the *Mouta* held another,
551. Close beside her dead son Zechen,
552. Gosla lifeless, ashen lay,
553. Inside the rock tomb dug by Zel.
   Assembly: Inside the rock tomb dug by Zel.

554. Clan of Marzuk gathered 'round them,
555. Each sad mourner cast two stones,
556. Purple stones that gave protection,
557. From the spirits of the night.
   Assembly: From the spirits of the night.

Casting the purple stones

558. Two logs of *tasou-tet* were cut,
559. Placed nearby her head and feet,
560. Upon the grave they piled the *hashab*,
561. Made from woven leaves of palm.
   Assembly: Made from woven leaves of palm.

562. With his eyes both wet and clouded,
563. Zel took hold of Marzuk's hand,
564. They walked the winding path together,
565. Towards their home and empty hearth.
   Assembly: Towards their home and empty hearth.

566. Never more a Queen's fine laughter,
567. Never more a mother's singing,
568. Night's damp darkness swirled about them,
569. Night's damp cold a heavy burden,
    Assembly: Night's damp cold a heavy burden.

570. Towards their home they walked in silence,
571. Eyes downcast along the way,
572. Both had lost: a wife—a mother,
573. No more their lives would be the same.
    Assembly: No more their lives would be the same.

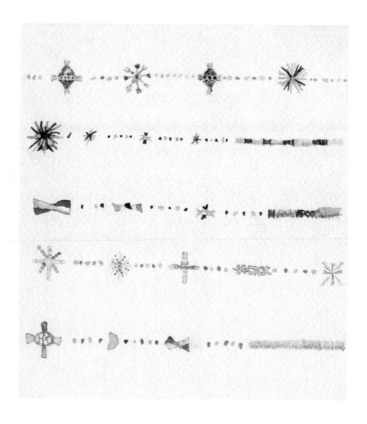

The First Elder rises and recites . . . [Lines 574-669].

Taw-lid

574. *Marzuk ar-baat fas-l ba'd,*
575. *Qaren Gurzel yeh-sel Zel.*
576. *Kel-et ibno Zel le-qauwih,*
577. *Hukm 'ad-dil kul-e naas.*
    Za'qikla: *Hukm 'ad-dil kul-e naas.*

Genealogy

574. Marzuk died four seasons later,
575. *Gurzel's* horns passed on to Zel,
576. Zel's son Kel-et strong of body,
577. His reign was fair to one and all.
    Assembly: His reign was fair to one and all.

578. Two Kingships later under Thelt,
579. While hunting towards the setting sun,
580. Found bluish stones the clan called *kpr*,
581. *Kpr* stones that could break flint.
    Assembly: *Kpr* stones that could break flint.

582. From one elder came the thought that,
583. *Kpr* stones might make a knife,
584. One that would not snap on bone,
585. When cutting meat for clan to eat.
    Assembly: When cutting meat for clan to eat.

586. Seasons passed and then generations,
587. Came the time when one-eyed Theno,
588. Bound together toughened skins,
589. That captured in his bag the wind.
     Assembly: That captured in his bag the wind.

590. Theno fanned his burning embers,
591. Until they glowed a fiery white,
592. Metal flowed from bluish stones,
593. He mined in secret through the night.
     Assembly: He mined in secret through the night.

594. Fen the white-haired King of Siwa,
595. Twelve times distant from King Marzuk,
596. Gave to Theno and his family,
597. Full possession of the mines.
     Assembly: Full possession of the mines.

598. Theno worked the hardened metal,
599. Formed it into blades of beauty,
600. Some with gentle curving arcs,
601. Knives reflecting noon-day sun.
     Assembly: Knives reflecting noon-day sun.

602. Each day found the valley peaceful,
603. Man the hunter, wife the mother,
604. Joyful life within the Siwa,
605. Filled with sounds of children singing.
     Assembly: Filled with sounds of children singing.

606. Happy years the reign of Feron,
607. He the mate of smiling Benta,
608. She gave birth four seasons later,
609. To a daughter then a son.
     Assembly: To a daughter then a son.

610. Chnt the wise would follow next,
611. In the footsteps of the Kings,
612. Ork then Dalben then another,
613. Darv the younger wise and able.
    Assembly: Darv the younger wise and able.

614. Darv while hunting found a plant that,
615. Caught his eye and gave good taste,
616. He told others who would ponder,
617. How the plant could help the clan.
    Assembly: How the plant could help the clan.

618. A plant that grew throughout the year,
619. One that needed little tending,
620. A plant that filled the families' stomachs,
621. When the hunters found no game.
    Assembly: When the hunters found no game.

622. Elders with more time to ponder,
623. Twice removed from time of Darv,
624. Brought about new changing ways,
625. For with leisure men could think.
    Assembly: For with leisure men could think.

626. Yet the tribe was slow to change,
627. Feeling strong that life was better,
628. Than in the time of distant brothers,
629. For to change could be disruptive.
    Assembly: For to change could be disruptive.

630. Elders spoke that plants were needed,
631. If the ranging herds of meat-beasts,
632. Ever left the Siwa valley,
633. Still they made no firm decision.
    Assembly: Still they made no firm decision.

634. Others spoke that if the clan would,
635. Tend the fields of *tamzooah,*
636. Hunting urges would decline and,
637. Men would lose their skills as hunters.
    Assembly: Men would lose their skills as hunters.

638. Others spoke that both were needed,
639. Let the fields of *tamzooah* grow,
640. While the young and able hunters,
641. Could provide the meat for all.
    Assembly: Could provide the meat for all.

642. Seasons passed then generations,
643. Still there was no firm decision,
644. Then King Gmena son of Tollek,
645. He proclaimed a work division.
    Assembly: Proclaimed a work division.

646. Lines of hunters would continue—
647. Side by side with men of planting—
648. Ended were the doubtful times and,
649. Worry if the herds would come.
    Assembly: Worry if the herds would come.

650. Came new times within the Siwa,
651. Fields of *tamzooah* now flourished,
652. Other clansmen planted *muchan,*
653. *Eefilan* and still others *yardin.*
    Assembly: *Eefilan* and still others *yardin.*

654. Each week hunters brought the meat,
655. Gained through stealth and tracking skills,
656. Hunters—planters worked together,
657. Sharing food within the clan.
    Assembly: Sharing food within the clan.

658. Lines of Kingship flowed to sons,
659. Peaceful passed the horns of *Gurzel*,
660. Until the reign of young King Valdes,
661. When his actions caused despair.
     Assembly: When his actions caused despair.

662. Valdes heeded not *Zagilie*,
663. Broke the promise of Queen Gosla.
664. Left the sacred flame untended,
665. Deep inside *Aghourmi's* temple,
     Assembly: Deep inside *Aghourmi's* temple,

Temple flame left untended

666. Four suns passed with flame extinguished,
667. No light shown down from temple mount,
668. High above *Zagilie* saw how,
669. King Valdes had brought dishonor.
     Assembly: King Valdes had brought dishonor.

The Second Elder rises and recites . . . [Lines 670-861].

Saq-qah

670. *Sha-trah Falil ibno Valdes,*
671. *Qaren Gurzel yeh-sel Taz.*
672. *Taz ba-Fanna—bad-ain Tauk,*
673. *Ho'eh bad-ain yeh-sel Beldn.*
   Za'qikla: *Ho'eh bad-ain yeh-sel Beldn.*

Schism

670. Valdes' son the clever Falil,
671. Passed *Gurzel's* horns to his son Taz,
672. Taz to Fanna—then to Tauk,
673. Who in turn anointed Beldn.
   Assembly: Who in turn anointed Beldn.

Beldn wearing the horns of Gurzel

674. Beldn's son the smiling Tsnet,
675. Died before his test of manhood,
676. From a fall that broke his body,
677. Leaving not an heir for Kingship.
   Assembly: Leaving not an heir for Kingship.

678. Beldn filled with pain and sadness,
679. Lost his caution in the hunt,
680. Fell victim to a *farna* beast that,
681. Leaped down from its hidden den.
   Assembly: Leaped down from its hidden den.

682. For the first time in the Siwa,
683. Marzuk's clan was without leader,
684. People feared now for their future,
685. There was no link to Marzuk's past.
       Assembly: There was no link to Marzuk's past.

686. Clansmen feared that good Queen Zena,
687. Might not take for husband, Tella,
688. Beldn's brother without wife,
689. As required by laws of clan.
       Assembly: As required by laws of clan.

690. When the time for union came,
691. And all had gathered at *Aghourmi,*
692. Tella spoke kind words of Beldn,
693. How his rule was just for all.
       Assembly: How his rule was just for all.

694. Tella offered Zena honor,
695. Respectful words to brother's wife,
696. How they both could make a child,
697. To keep alive the line of promise.
       Assembly: To keep alive the line of promise.

698. Tella offered unto Zena,
699. Dressed in black with sunburst showing,
700. Honor—if but she agree,
701. To take him to her hearth and bed.
       Assembly: To take him to her hearth and bed.

702. All assembled watched in silence,
703. Awaiting Zena's words to Tella,
704. Words that she would honor Bella,
705. Take his brother for her mate.
       Assembly: Take his brother for her mate.

706. As tears streamed slowly down her face,
707. From under Zena's sunburst dress,
708. She grasped a hidden copper knife,
709. One she carried for protection.
    Assembly: One she carried for protection.

710. Before the gathered clan of Marzuk,
711. She raised the knife for all to see—
712. Before a hand could stay its course,
713. She plunged the knife into her breast.
    Assembly: She plunged the knife into her breast.

714. Dying Zena's words were heart-felt,
715. Bella's death had brought her sorrow,
716. With Bella's death her life was empty,
717. Darkness was all she could see.
    Assembly: Darkness was all she could see.

718. Zena pleaded for forgiveness,
719. Zena felt no ill towards Tella,
720. Only endless love for Beldn,
721. He her mate and constant lover.
    Assembly: He her mate and constant lover.

722. As the cloak of death drew closer,
723. Zena tried to speak once more—
724. But at that moment spirit left her,
725. Leaving Zena's words unspoken.
    Assembly: Leaving Zena's words unspoken.

726. Tella sought the elder Vana,
727. Oldest of the speaking men,
728. How were they to choose a King,
729. When line of Marzuk had been severed?
    Assembly: When line of Marzuk had been severed?

730. When the sun had risen twice,
731. Vana called the clan assemble,
732. They must choose from all the men,
733. A leader to become their King.
     Assembly: A leader to become their King.

734. How should the Kingship line continue,
735. Through the sister of Queen Zena?
736. Should the Kingship pass through Tella,
737. Beldn's brother now alone?
     Assembly: Beldn's brother now alone?

738. Some elders saw another choice,
739. One of strength, a test of valor,
740. He the strongest—he the boldest,
741. Only he should wear the horns.
     Assembly: Only he should wear the horns.

741. Disputed rival family claims,
743. Voices 'round the fire whispered,
744. Should their future be with one whose,
745. Strength was greatest in the valley?
     Assembly: Strength was greatest in the valley?

746. The strongest he had fought wild beasts,
747. He the strongest able hunter,
748. Such a man could not be Tella,
749. But could only be Ferzin.
     Assembly: But could only be Ferzin.

750. Born of Khal and his mate Dezna,
751. Lean of body swift of foot,
752. Ferzin with the strength of heroes,
753. He could lead the clan of Marzuk.
     Assembly: He could lead the clan of Marzuk.

754. But was not Ferzin a puzzle?
755. Ever prideful, ever boasting?
756. He of easy rising anger?
757. Would Ferzin be wise as Tella?
   Assembly: Would Ferzin be wise as Tella?

758. Long they pondered through day,
759. Long into the night past dawn,
760. At *Aghourmi* temple gathered,
761. Men of Siwa made their choice.
   Assembly: Men of Siwa made their choice.

762. Varna wisest of the elders,
763. Stood and told their ancient story,
764. How coming from the ice-bound land,
765. Marzuk's clan had found the Siwa.
   Assembly: Marzuk's clan had found the Siwa.

766. Varna wisest of the elders,
767. Recited words of sacred pledge,
768. Made by Gosla to *Zagilie*,
769. Reminding all of Valdes' shame.
   Assembly: Reminding all of Valdes' shame.

770. Varna wisest of the elders,
771. Spoke to all the men assembled:
772. *The time is now to make your choice,*
773. *Make it wisely one and all.*
   Assembly: Make it wisely one and all.

774. Each man with a beard then stood,
775. Each who passed his test of manhood,
776. Each who passed his test of hunting,
777. They would choose the clan's new King.
   Assembly: They would choose the clan's new King.

778. All agreed the choice be binding,
779. Those against could leave the Siwa,
780. If they would not allegiance give,
781. To the King—the chosen one.
     Assembly: To the King—the chosen one.

782. One by one each made their choice,
783. Casting different colored stones,
784. The count was such that few chose Tella,
785. Brother of respected Beldn.
     Assembly: Brother of respected Beldn.

786. The count was such that most the Siwans,
787. Stood behind the hunter Ferzin,
788. Save for thirty-two that stood,
789. In downcast silence behind Tella.
     Assembly: In downcast silence behind Tella.

790. Marzuk's clan had made their choice,
791. Each man in his separate way,
792. Most had chosen strength, not reason,
793. Horns of *Gurzel* passed to Ferzin
     Assembly: Horns of *Gurzel* passed to Ferzin.

794. Friends of Tella gathered 'round him,
795. Met in council through the night,
796. A chill of cold embraced their bodies,
797. Racing heartbeats echoed loud.
     Assembly: Racing heartbeats echoed loud.

798. From the shadows came a sound,
799. As when hunters stalk wild game,
800. Lifting up their eyes they gazed,
801. Upon the chosen King of Siwa.
     Assembly: Upon the chosen King of Siwa.

802. Ferzin met their eyes with fire,
803. Speaking low with careful words:
804. *Stay and work with me my brothers,*
805. *There is place for all in Siwa.*
    Assembly: There is place for all in Siwa.

806. *Though you rejected me in choosing,*
807. *I proclaim a lasting truce.*
808. *Stay and work with me my brothers,*
809. *There is place for all in Siwa.*
    Assembly: There is place for all in Siwa.

810. But his eyes reflected danger,
811. That would follow if they stayed,
812. Night sounds ceased as Tella stood,
813. Turned, and faced the King of Siwa:
    Assembly: Turned, and faced the King of Siwa.

814. *We respect the choice of clan,*
815. *You are King within the Siwa,*
816. *Rule in justice, King Ferzin,*
817. *Place your faith in elders' council.*
    Assembly: Place your faith in elders' council.

818. *Keep our sacred symbols three,*
819. *Sunburst, disc, and horns of Gurzel.*
820. *We will leave and venture eastward,*
821. *For there can be just one leader.*
821. **Assembly:** For there can be just one leader.

822. Ferzin slipped out through the darkness,
823. Each heart knew the risk and danger,
824. They had chosen Tella leader,
825. King Ferzin would not forget.
    Assembly: King Ferzin would not forget.

826. With the dawn the men assembled,
827. Women brought them chests of reed,
828. Chests to carry eggs of *prnex*,
829. Eggs to hold their drinking water.
    Assembly: Eggs to hold their drinking water.

830. Others brought dried strips of meat,
831. For they knew not if the wild-beasts,
832. Would always follow them in travel,
833. So for food they would not want.
    Assembly: So for food they would not want.

834. When the light of dawn reflected,
835. From the salt-white temple walls,
836. Many gathered bid them safety,
837. For to conquer desert perils.
    Assembly: For to conquer desert perils.

838. Before the gathered Siwan elders,
839. Tella stood before King Ferzin,
840. Each to the other gave his hand,
841. Pledging honor and respect.
    Assembly: Pledging honor and respect.

842. Taking ancient knives of flint,
843. They slashed three times on up-turned palms,
844. Binding both to laws of clan,
845. Both to honor tribe and person.
    Assembly: Both to honor tribe and person.

846. As the cloak of temple shadow,
847. Covered both and sealed the pact,
848. The eyes of Ferzin closed and lowered,
849. Hid from all their hateful message.
    Assembly: Hid from all their hateful message.

850. Tella walked around *Aghourmi*,
851. Three times made the ritual passage,
852. Thirty-two with wives and children,
853. Towards the east began their march.
    Assembly: Towards the east began their march.

854. Parting drained the human spirit,
855. Eyes of many damp with tears,
856. Trust and hope were placed with Tella,
857. Marchers chanted songs of glory.
    Assembly: Marchers chanted songs of glory.

858. Through the ever growing darkness,
859. Slinked the new-crowned King of Siwa,
860. Eyes ablaze reflecting madness,
861. Plotting death for Tella's band.
    Assembly: Plotting death for Tella's band.

The Third Elder rises and recites . . . [Lines 862-925].

Qara

862. *Bib-uth etsal-laq es-sad,*
863. *Wahd-bi-wahd ihti-ras gradt,*
864. *Af-tlh hag-ar kbire zhol-ka,*
865. *Reg-glem ew-ga—ad-rum ta'ban.*
     Za'qikla: *Reg-glem ew-ga—ad-rum ta'ban.*

Qara

862. Slowly they ascended climbing,
863. One by one with careful steps,
864. Over boulders up the scarp,
865. Legs were aching—arms were tired.
     Assembly: Legs were aching—arms were tired.

866. Halfway up the rocks they rested,
867. Allowing time to ease their spirits,
868. Tired elders, women, children,
869. Sat and rested in the shade.
     Assembly: Sat and rested in the shade.

870. Restored bodies offered prayers,
871. *God Zagilie give us strength,*
872. *We have left the Siwa valley,*
873. *Guide us to a new-found land.*
     Assembly: Guide us to a new-found land.

874.   *Grant us in the coming dawns that,*
875.   *We will find a welcome home,*
876.   *Where we can live in peace and prosper,*
877.   *With no fear from Ferzin's rule.*
       Assembly: With no fear from Ferzin's rule.

878.   After seven dawns had risen,
879.   High and crossed the bluish heaven,
880.   Tella stood along the cliff that,
881.   Overlooked a winding valley.
       Assembly: Overlooked a winding valley.

882.   Rocks with strange configurations,
883.   Rose up from the valley floor,
884.   Like ancient eerie night-time spirits,
885.   Thus he named the valley Qara.
       Assembly: Thus he named the valley Qara.

886.   Near the center of the Qara,
887.   Next to a rising mound of stone,
888.   Tella found a *taut* of sweetness,
889.   There the people placed their hearths.
       Assembly: There the people placed their hearths.

890.   Seasons passed and then more seasons,
891.   Tella took for mate young Marla,
892.   Many feast-fires marked their union,
893.   Giving hope for future sons.
       Assembly: Giving hope for future sons.

894.   But when her birthing time was due,
895.   Came not a boy but laughing girl,
896.   People waited and they chanted:
897.   *God Zagilie grant a son!*
       Assembly: God *Zagilie* grant a son!

898. When five seasons more had passed,
899. A second daughter Marla bore,
900. People waited and they chanted:
901. *God Zagilie, grant a son!*
   Assembly: God *Zagilie* grant a son!

902. Marla bore harsh barbs of laughter,
903. When she passed among the women,
904. Words that echoed through the Qara,
905. *God Zagilie grant a son!*
   Assembly: God *Zagilie* grant a son!

906. One year later came new movement,
907. Stirring wildly in her belly,
908. Growing stronger every day,
909. Soon a son lay by her side.
   Assembly: Soon a son lay by her side.

910. Jubilation—celebration,
911. Happy feasting filled the Qara,
912. *Zagilie* cast his hand upon them,
913. Tella's band had honored god.
   Assembly: Tella's band had honored god.

914. Marla covered new son Rak,
915. With warming pelts from desert *farna,*
916. Happy seasons were upon them,
917. In the peaceful Qara valley.
   Assembly: In the peaceful Qara valley.

918. Seasons passed and then more seasons,
919. Out from the desert, from the west,
920. Came two men with blistered skins,
921. With words of pain they begged for food.
   Assembly: With words of pain they begged for food.

Arrival of the strangers at Gara

83

922. Who were these men with broken bodies?
923. Who were these men with pleading eyes?
924. Who were these men who braved the desert?
925. Who were these men now in the Qara?
    Assembly: Who were these men now in the Qara?

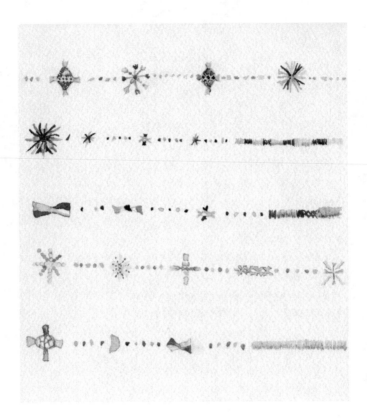

The Fourth Elder rises and recites . . . [Lines 926-1017].

Ha-ga'l

926. *Tella tahya Gar-be 'etnin,*
927. *Daoud weh' Lez qnt sa'b m'shadu,*
928. *Wish-em gda'af her-ak sham-si,*
929. *Isaratat sa-anah muhif.*
   Za'qikla: *Isaratat sa-anagh muhif.*

Shame

926. Tella greeted both the strangers,
927. Daoud and Lez were friends not foes,
928. Their blistered sun-burnt fissured faces,
929. Bore the signs of fearful times.
   Assembly: Bore the signs of fearful times.

930. Banished were they sent to wander,
931. Ten days without food or water,
932. Left to die the choking death,
933. When tongues of men turned dry and black.
   Assembly: When tongues of men turned dry and black.

934. After both had drunk and eaten,
935. Passed three dawns in fitful sleep,
936. Qara men gathered around them,
937. For to hear their kinsmen's tale.
   Assembly: For to hear their kinsmen's tale.

938. Qara men sat hushed and quiet,
939. Silence swept across the valley,
940. Even night-time *tzesia* failed to,
941. Fill the evening with their sounds.
Assembly: Fill the evening with their sounds.

942. Daoud and Lez each told their stories,
943. Of the madness of King Ferzin,
944. Who threw a lamp of *zeitun* oil,
945. That burned *Zagilie's* sacred gifts.
Assembly: That burned *Zagilie's* sacred gifts.

946. *Aghourmi's* temple walls had crumbled,
947. Falling from their rocky height,
948. Smashed and broken stones now lay,
949. In shapeless piles upon the ground.
Assembly: In shapeless piles upon the ground.

950. Came next a day when noon-time blackened,
951. When sun disk vanished from the sky,
952. All the valley sighed and shuddered,
953. Terror reigned throughout the Siwa.
Assembly: Terror reigned throughout the Siwa.

954. Then God *Zagilie* in his wrath,
955. Took from Siwa all the meat-beasts,
956. For six long months the family hunters,
957. Returned empty without food.
Assembly: Returned empty without food.

958. Meat once saved from other seasons,
959. Stores of food that once eased hunger,
960. Ferzin came in dark of night,
961. He stole the food for his own use.
Assembly: He stole the food for his own use.

962. When all Siwan elders gathered,
963. We spoke out against the King,
964. Ferzin seized us, roughly bound us,
965. Gave us to his lustful followers.
    Assembly: Gave us to his lustful followers.

966. We felt the anguish pain of hatred,
967. Felt the ropes against our throats,
968. Felt the cuts they made upon us,
969. Felt their *yatouss* up inside us.
    Assembly: Felt their *yatouss* up inside us.

970. Soon they tired of their games,
971. Our captors laughed, we then were taken,
972. To a cave above lake *Berka*,

Siwans being tortured

973. Imprisoned there for many nights.
    Assembly: Imprisoned there for many nights.

974. Lez, my brother, both together,
975. We spoke the truth defied Ferzin,
976. In our cave of filth and cold,
977. We were together not alone.
    Assembly: We were together not alone.

978. Then came men in masks and took us,
979. Brought us forth before the King,
980. Ferzin ordered men to strip us,
981. He would satisfy his lust.
    Assembly: He would satisfy his lust.

982. We were lashed with leather strips,
983. Forced to lie upon the ground,
984. Ferzin's men took liquid *malah*,
985. Smeared the salt upon our wounds.
    Assembly: Smeared the salt upon our wounds.

986. We were scourged, declared outcast,
987. None to help or render aid,
988. Should any offer outstretched hand,
989. Ferzin swore that they would die.
    Assembly: Ferzin swore that they would die.

990. Forced were we out from the Siwa,
991. Forced to start a life of hiding,
992. Forced to flee from our own brothers,
993. Forced to live like hunted beasts!
    Assembly: Forced to live like hunted beasts!

994. We were driven from our Siwa,
995. Without food or cooling water,
996. Fate would guide us to you Tella,
997. Now our lives are in your hands.
    Assembly: Now our lives are in your hands.

998. Light from the council fire glowed,
999. Showed the Qarans deep in thought,
1000. Around the cracking spitting embers,
1001. Muffled words rose up in hate.
    Assembly: Muffled words rose up in hate.

1002. Ferzin had betrayed the Siwa,
1003. Broken Gosla's sacred promise,
1004. But the Qarans were not many,
1005. But thirty-two had made the journey.
    Assembly: But thirty-two had made the journey.

1006. Later seasons saw six others,
1007. Pass successful rites of manhood,
1008. Now the two outcasts from Siwa,
1009. Swelled their numbers now to forty.
    Assembly: Swelled their numbers now to forty.

1010. Forty men now pledged their honor,
1011. Each man from the Qara stood:
1012. Thrust his spear unto the heavens,
1013. Pledged their lives in sacred trust.
     Assembly: Pledged their lives in sacred trust.

1014. Men united—giving hope,
1015. Men united—standing strong,
1016. Men united—would prevail,
1017. Men united—marched to Siwa!
     Assembly: Men united—marched to Siwa!

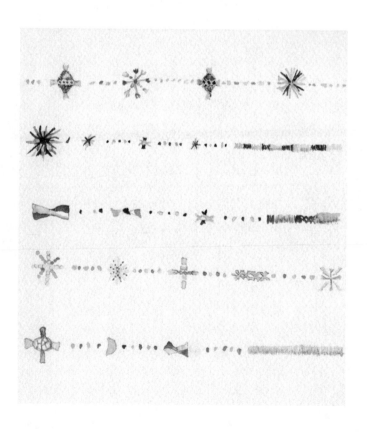

The Fifth Elder rises and recites . . . [Lines 1018-1085].

Mara-sakt Mah-ht

1018. *Kas'saf-alein gam-b'al* zhol-ka,
1019. *Sh'ft al-Gayum ram-malat,*
1020. *Gar-ri bilna q'li Ferzin,*
1021. *Rag-l ar-ba'reen ma-ra-kaat.*
    Za'qikla: *Rag-l ar-ba'reen ma-ra-kaat.*

Death Duel

1018. Siwan scouts along the scarp,
1019. Tracked the moving clouds of dust,
1020. Quickly ran and told Ferzin,
1021. Forty men had come for battle.
    Assembly: Forty men had come for battle.

1022. West of Aghourmi's temple stones,
1023. Where hooded *eli-feing* lived,
1024. Men from Qara set their camp,
1025. Awaited Ferzin and his band.
    Assembly: Awaited Ferzin and his band.

1026. Tella, King of eastern Qara,
1027. Face to face with King Ferzin,
1028. Words were hurled across the clearing,
1029. Ancient words of death-duel challenge.
    Assembly: Ancient words of death-duel challenge.

1030. Ferzin lunged his muscles gleaming,
1031. Both men gripped their hunting knives,
1032. Madness glowed from Ferzin's eyes,
1033. Eyes that gazed like night-time *bouma*.
   Assembly: Eyes that gazed like night-time *bouma*.

1034. Both men rushed towards one another,
1035. Feinting, lunging seeking weakness,
1036. Ever cautious feinting, lunging,
1037. He that erred would find quick death.
   Assembly: He that erred would find quick death.

1038. Ferzin slashed and blood spilled out,
1039. Across the blade arm of King Tella,
1040. Tella lunged in graceful motion,
1041. Slit the chest of Ferzin deep.
   Assembly: Slit the chest of Ferzin deep.

1042. Blood flowed down his muscled body,
1043. Trickled down across his belly,
1044. From Ferzin's dust-parched throat emerged,
1045. A sound, a scream of beast-like fury.
   Assembly: A sound, a scream of beast-like fury.

1046. Leaping, lunging like the *farna,*
1047. Ferzin sent King Tella sprawling,
1048. Tella's hand still held his knife,
1049. But his fall had snapped the blade.
   Assembly: But his fall had snapped the blade.

1050. Ferzin's mouth curved with a smile,
1051. The Siwan King closed for the kill,
1052. Ferzin screamed four words at Tella,
1053. *Ahdo ka-i al-E ifsa.*
   Assembly: Ahdo ka-i al-E ifsa.

1054. Standing o'er the fallen Tella,
1055. Loomed the maddened form of Ferzin,
1056. Tella turned and saw a glimmer,
1057. Amid the fallen temple stones—
    Assembly: Amid the fallen temple stones—

1058. A glint—a sacred copper knife,
1059. An ancient gift to god *Zagilie*,
1060. Former god the clan had worshiped,
1061. Former god the clan once honored.
    Assembly: Former god the clan once honored.

1062. Loomed the grinning face of Ferzin,
1063. Filled with raging evil lust,
1064. Ferzin screamed, saw not the danger,
1065. Blinded by his rising fury.
    Assembly: Blinded by his rising fury.

1066. He saw not the copper knife that,
1067. Tella grasped within his hand,
1068. As Ferzin lunged to end the fight,
1069. *Zagalie* guided Tella's blade.
    Assembly: *Zagalie* guided Tella's blade.

1070. King Ferzin's eyes showed disbelief,
1071. A look of doubt crept o'er his face,
1072. The guiding hand of god *Zagilie*,
1073. Drove the blade into his heart.
    Assembly: Drove the blade into his heart.

1074. A copper knife—a gift to god,
1075. Determined who would live or die,
1076. But how this knife had reappeared,
1077. Upon the earth at proper time—?
    Assembly: Upon the earth at proper time—?

The copper knife

1078. All Siwa men were left to ponder,
1079. How *Zagilie* favored Tella,
1080. Tella offered words of friendship,
1081. Amid the cheering gathered clansmen.
   Assembly: Amid the cheering gathered clansmen.

1082. Men carried Ferzin to the *Mouta*,
1083. But none would offer ancient blessings,
1084. None would cast the purple stones,
1085. Ferzin in short time was forgotten.
   Assembly: Ferzin in short time was forgotten.

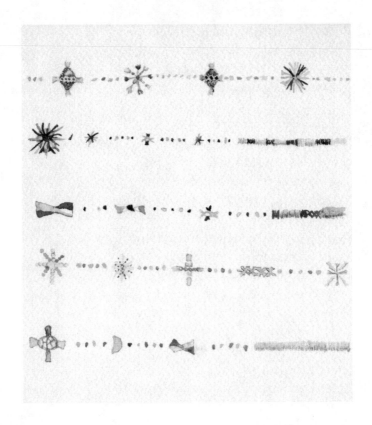

The First Elder rises and recites . . . [Lines 1086-1169].

Zukerdahla

1086. *Tella bin-ya' ha-ma'badd*
1087. *Fu-qal tul-uh al-Aghourmi,*
1088. *Gau-want sanduq muad'desha,*
1089. *Sil na's saq-kena Zagilie.*
     Za'qikla: *Sil na's saq-kena Zagilie.*

Transition

1086. Tella built again the temple,
1087. Rising high above *Aghourmi,*
1088. Inside the god's own sacred chest,
1089. He placed *Zagilie's* copper knife.
     Assembly: He placed *Zagilie's* copper knife.

1090. Tella ruled the Siwa justly,
1091. Giving way to his son Rak,
1092. Rak to Peno—then to Mela,
1093. Then to Kala—on to Blert.
     Assembly: Then to Kala—on to Blert.

1094. In the reign of Blert's son Tola,
1095. Grew a clouded sense of time,
1096. How should the clan re-count the seasons,
1097. How to remember ancient Kings?
     Assembly: How to remember ancient Kings?

1098. Around the council fires they chanted,
1099. Different lists of Kings and heroes,
1100. Stories changing by the season,
1101. Some names added others lost.
    Assembly: Some names added others lost.

1102. No two lists of ancient Kings,
1103. Were alike in name or sequence,
1104. Stories of their famous heroes,
1105. Became legends of great men.
    Assembly: Became legends of great men.

1106. Nobel traits of Siwan Kings,
1107. Added to the names of others,
1108. Making hero Kings of greatness,
1109. Who took their place among the gods.
    Assembly: Who took their place among the gods.

1110. To aged Plen the son of Tola,
1111. Came the thought of picture drawing,
1112. Others called his symbols useless,
1113. Just to carve them took much time.
    Assembly: Just to carve them took much time.

1114. Clansmen thought it not important,
1115. That a record should be made,
1116. The clan had changed much for the better,
1117. Ancient deeds seemed old and useless.
    Assembly: Ancient deeds seemed old and useless.

1118. Elders saw in their own lifetimes,
1119. Many better useful changes,
1120. Working metal, weaving, cooking,
1121. Carving wood for daily use.
    Assembly: Carving wood for daily use.

1122. Yet one change was still neglected,
1123. How to leave a lasting memory,
1124. How to send the thoughts of clansmen,
1125. From the present to the future?
    Assembly: From the present to the future?

1126. Youthful Benis when a lad,
1127. Found a tiny *o-gar-azee*,
1128. Near the body of its mother,
1129. Took the beast and gave it care.
    Assembly: Took the beast and gave it care.

1130. Benis and his *o-gar-azee*,
1131. Played together in the valley,
1132. Benis named the beast *Sal-Lukie*,
1133. Name that meant the *Swiftest Wind*.
    Assembly: Name that meant the *Swiftest Wind*.

Saluki hunting dogs

1134. Endless days in joy they ran,
1135. Across the valley two as one,
1136. But came a time *Sal-Lukie* changed,
1137. Took once again to savage ways.
    Assembly: Took once again to savage ways.

1138. But *Sal-Lukie* did not vanish,
1139. Season after season saw him,
1140. Running side by side with hunters,
1141. Giving aid to Siwa men.
    Assembly: Giving aid to Siwa men.

1142. Elders pondered was it right,
1143. For men to befriend desert beasts,
1144. Might a day come when *Sal-Lukie*,
1145. Harmed a child and all bear guilt?
Assembly: Harmed a child and all bear guilt.

1146. Seasons passed then generations,
1147. Horns of *Gurzel* passed to others,
1148. Minds grew clever, thoughts were heeded,
1149. Men turned to nature for their use.
Assembly: Men turned to nature for their use.

1150. Tort the younger found new metal,
1151. That when mixed with shiny copper,
1152. Gave more hardness to their blades,
1153. Made such blades last seasons longer.
Assembly: Made such blades last seasons longer.

1154. Some made pots from different earths,
1155. Than had their fathers in the past,
1156. Some made pots baked hard by fire,
1157. That held water through the night.
Assembly: That held water through the night.

1158. Siwans changed their tools and weapons,
1159. Found new ways to harvest plants,
1160. Siwans tamed the beast *Sal-Lukie*,
1161. Made the beast serve needs of man.
Assembly: Made the beast serve needs of man.

1162. Clansmen chose their lines of work,
1163. Sons followed fathers in their footsteps,
1164. Farmers, hunters, potters, weavers,
1165. All together in the Siwa.
Assembly: All together in the Siwa.

1166. Relet's son took *Gurzel's* horns,
1167. Clansmen flourished as before,
1168. But in his rule there came the time,
1169. When strangers entered Siwa valley.
Assembly: When strangers entered Siwa valley.

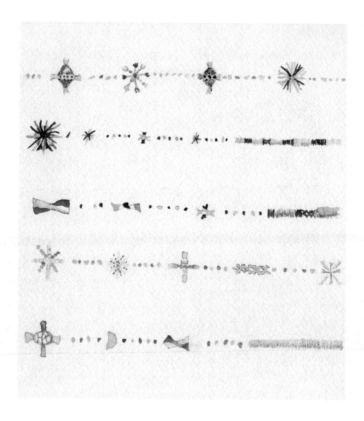

The Second Elder rises and recites . . . [Lines 1170-1321].

Te-Henu

1170. *Sai'yad-detu gan-wah Siwa,*
1171. *Ul-litum hiwagh zeh rhigal,*
1172. *Sai'yad-detu ehsas gura-bah,*
1173. *Dayman gan-set—dayman raqib.*
    Za'qikla: *Dayman gan-set—dayman raqib.*

Te-Henu

1170. Hunters tracking in the Siwa,
1171. Reported seeing man-like forms,
1172. Hunters sensed new strangers present,
1173. Ever stalking—ever watching.
    Assembly: Ever stalking—ever watching.

1174. Some elders thought these man-like forms,
1175. Were spirits of dead Siwan Kings,
1176. Returned to hunt the running *izm,*
1177. As before in former lives.
    Assembly: As before in former lives.

1178. King Whelk son of able Relet,
1179. Knew the forms not ancient spirits,
1180. He had seen not one but many,
1181. Ever lurking in the shadows.
    Assembly: Ever lurking in the shadows.

1182. Whelk assembled all the hunters,
1183. *We must be ready, ever ready,*
1184. Whelk commanded—*be prepared,*
1185. *These strangers may not come in peace.*
    Assembly: These strangers may not come in peace.

1186. Seasons passed and then more seasons,
1187. Strangers watching from afar,
1188. Strangers stood more boldly open,
1189. As if wanting to be seen.
    Assembly: As if wanting to be seen.

1190. Sunset cast its long dark shadows,
1191. Out across the valley floor,
1192. From the west there came a cry:
1193. They are coming—strangers coming!
    Assembly: They are coming—strangers coming!

1194. Whelk assembled all the hunters,
1195. Send the children to their mothers,
1196. Hide the women for protection,
1197. We will march to meet the strangers.
    Assembly: We will march to meet the strangers.

1198. Against the skyline stood the strangers,
1199. Dressed in finest woven clothing,
1200. Leather straps about their arms,
1201. Draping down their sun-tanned thighs.
    Assembly: Draping down their sun-tanned thighs.

1202. Strangers wore headbands of
    feathers,
1203. From the giant birds called *ipix,*
1204. Feathers that gave rise to
    murmurs,
1205. That the strangers came in
    peace.
    Assembly: That the strangers
    came in peace.

Arrival of the Tehenu

1206. Each stranger held two spears of wood,
1207. Tipped with shiny blackened blades,
1208. Metal strange and unlike any,
1209. Seen inside the Siwa valley.
   Assembly: Seen inside the Siwa valley.

1210. Whelk advanced, made signs of peace,
1211. Spoke to the strangers words of welcome,
1212. Wrmr leader of the strangers,
1213. Spoke to Whelk in words familiar—
   Assembly: Spoke to Whelk in words familiar—

1214. *We are Te-Henu from the north lands,*
1215. *We are Te-Henu distant brothers,*
1216. *Both our clans are linked by blood,*
1217. *We from Marzuk's younger brother.*
   Assembly: They from Marzuk's younger brother.

1218. Wrmr spoke kind words of greeting,
1219. Told Whelk of their distant past,
1220. Told of a time when Kings of Siwa,
1221. Once had lived within the Qara.
   Assembly: Once had lived within the Qara.

1222. Wrmr spoke how long ago,
1223. Men from the Qara traveled northward,
1224. Met their Te-Henu brothers living,
1225. Close beside the sea of *Vanton.*
   Assembly: Close beside the sea of *Vanton.*

1226. Marzuk had a younger brother,
1227. Talgo, he, they called the lame,
1228. Talgo's clan stayed near the sea,
1229. While Marzuk led his people inland.
   Assembly: While Marzuk led his people inland.

1230. So it was the Te-Henu—Siwans,
1231. Were just distant clans of brothers,
1232. Strangers but with roots of family,
1233. United through the mists of time.
    Assembly: United through the mists of time.

1234. Though they lived in separate places,
1235. With a language somewhat different,
1236. They shared bonds of kin and friendship,
1237. Te-Henu—Siwans now united.
    Assembly: Te-Henu—Siwans now united.

1238. Wrmr spoke, *We come in peace,*
1239. *Good King Whelk you are my brother,*
1240. *Agree to let us form a bond,*
1241. *Together we can help each other.*
    Assembly: Together they could help each other.

1242. Thus the two clans merged together,
1243. Two as one, each gave the other,
1244. Ways of special daily living,
1245. How to hunt and how to share.
    Assembly: How to hunt and how to share.

1246. Te-Henu from the distant northlands,
1247. Shared their iron metal weapons,
1248. Siwans shared their crops of *yardin,*
1249. Growing well inside the valley.
    Assembly: Growing well inside the valley.

1250. From this union both clans flourished,
1251. Stone and metal tools were shared,
1252. New exciting concepts blended,
1253. Grew the peoples wiser stronger.
    Assembly: Grew the peoples wiser stronger.

1254. Sons of both Kings lived like brothers,
1255. Each one shared the hearth of other,
1256. Bonds of blood made both clans stronger,
1257. Siwans—Te-Henu brothers equal.
   Assembly: Siwans—Te-Henu brothers equal.

1258. Te-Henu—Siwans forged new weapons,
1259. Iron blades from rocks of red,
1260. Secrets learned six Kingships past,
1261. From eastern peoples called the Hittu.
   Assembly: From eastern peoples called the Hittu.

1262. In the Hittu mountain fortress,
1263. To the far north distant east,
1264. Hittu warriors made new weapons,
1265. From a new and hardened metal.
   Assembly: From a new and hardened metal.

1266. Hittu clans made war on Per-O,
1267. King of Chemi, sacred Black Land,
1268. Hittu blades turned edge of bronze,
1269. But numbers told the fate of war.
   Assembly: But numbers told the fate of war.

1270. Per-O drove the Hittu eastward,
1271. Sacked their homeland, now in ruins,
1272. But the secret of their metal,
1273. Had been learned by Te-Henu men.
   Assembly: Had been learned by Te-Henu men.

1274. Harsh new sounds within the Siwa,
1275. Blacksmiths pounded, forges rang,
1276. Smelting iron knives for thrusting,
1277. Making swords—the tools of war.
   Assembly: Making swords—the tools of war.

1278. Slowly peace had left the Siwa,
1279. But Te-Henu—Siwans did not know,
1280. Both clans saw a better life,
1281. With ideas much improved.
     Assembly: With ideas much improved.

1282. Friendship bonds with distant brothers,
1283. Families merged grew ever stronger,
1284. Soon the young men wanted more,
1285. Soon the young men cried—expand!
     Assembly: Soon the young men cried—expand!

1286. Whelk's oldest son, the strong Clearchus,
1287. Bore his father to the *Mouta*,
1288. Where both clans cast purple stones,
1289. Never knowing peace had left them.
     Assembly: Never knowing peace had left them.

1290. Young Clearchus carved a stele,
1291. Placed it in *Aghormie* temple,
1292. A stele with long lines of symbols,
1293. Telling of the feats of Kings:
     Assembly: Telling of the feats of Kings.

1294. Whelk the first—the mighty King—
1295. Whelk the first—who founded Siwa—
1296. Whelk the first—who joined with Te-Henu—
1297. Whelk the first—who forged an army—
     Assembly: Whelk the first—who forged an army—

1298. Clearchus read line after line:
1299. Clearchus—he who ruled the Siwa—
1300. Clearchus—he the greatest King—
1301. Clearchus—he the son of Whelk—
     Assembly: Clearchus—he the son of Whelk—

1302. How the people praised Clearchus,
1303. He had made them strong and able:
1304. Now they shouted: *Conquer Chem—*
1305. *To the Black Land—to the Black Land.*
    Assembly: To the Black Land—to the Black land.

1306. How the people praised Clearchus,
1307. Chanting words throughout the night:
1308. *We the strong—we are the mighty,*
1309. *We are Siwans—we are Te-Henu.*
    Assembly: We are Siwans—we are Te-Henu.

1310. Thoughts of peace had taken flight,
1311. Siwans—Te-Henu armed for battle,
1312. Shouts of war grew loud with passion:
1313. *Mighty King Clearchus lead us.*
    Assembly: Mighty King Clearchus lead us.

1314. Elders wishing peace were silenced,
1315. Shouts of war drowned out their voices:
1316. *To the Black Land—To the Black Land,*
1317. *Mighty King Clearchus lead us.*
    Assembly: Mighty King Clearchus lead us.

1318. Through the day and through the night,
1319. Shouts were raised and voices screamed:
1320. *To the Black Land—To the Black Land,*
1321. *Mighty King, Clearchus lead us.*
    Assembly: Mighty King Clearchus lead us.

The Third Elder rises and recites . . . [Lines 1322-1457].

Marak-ka Wahid

1322. *Tah-re'sarna weh harga'la,*
1323. *Dahil wad'di nahar Chemi,*
1324. *Mun-la'shir a-shakeri,*
1325. *Fah'metna al-Chemi daif-el.*
    Za'qikla: *Fah'metna al-Chemi daif-el.*

Battle I

1322. Revolution and disorder,
1323. In the Chemi river valley,
1324. Gave support to Siwan warriors,
1325. For they sensed the Chemi weak.
    Assembly: For they sensed the Chemi weak.

1326. On the plain near *Vanton's* shore,
1327. Two armies poised, their leaders ready,
1328. Te-Henu—Siwans rushed on forward,
1329. To victory—their battle cry.
    Assembly: To victory—their battle cry.

1330. Per-O dark skinned King of Chemi,
1331. Named from one who ruled before him,
1332. Mer-En-Ptah the son of the Ramses,
1333. Held firm against the rushing hoard.
    Assembly: Held firm against the rushing hoard.

1334. Mer-En-Ptah the son of the Ramses,
1335. Hurled them back into the wasteland,
1336. Siwan sons were slain in battle,
1337. Clearchus tried but could not save them.
Assembly: Clearchus tried but could not save them.

1338. Surrounded by the troops of Per-O,
1339. Clearchus fought beside his soldiers,
1340. As tufted arrows found their mark,
1341. Clearchus fell and could not rise.
Assembly: Clearchus fell and could not rise.

1342. Desert warriors without leader,
1343. Turned and fled across the plain,
1344. Fleeing from the Per-O's army,
1345. Crying: *Save us—from the Chemi.*
Assembly: Crying: Save us from the Chemi.

1346. Racing chariots, sounds of fury,
1347. Horses charging—hoof beats pounding,
1348. Men and beasts the Per-O's army,
1349. Fell upon the Te-Henu—Siwans.
Assembly: Fell upon the Te-Henu—Siwans.

1350. Bound to the chariots churning wheels,
1351. Blades of hardened metal slashed,
1532. Tearing through the Te-Henu bones,
1353. Slicing through the Siwan limbs.
Assembly: Slicing through the Siwan limbs.

Chemi chariots rout the Siwans

1354. Those that dodged the blades of death,
1355. Fell beneath the flailing hoofs,
1356. Of once wild beasts tamed now to serve,
1357. Mangled bodies screamed their last.
Assembly: Mangled bodies screamed their last.

1358. A battle scene of death and dying,
1359. Screams of victory—cries of pain,
1360. Pero-O's soldiers raised the banner—
1361. Pero-O's flag of victory.
     Assembly: Per-O's flag of victory.

1362. Vengeful farmers rushed upon them,
1363. Stripped the bodies of the wounded,
1364. Farmers who had lost their fields,
1365. Farmers who had families ravished.
     Assembly: Farmers who had families ravished.

1366. Vengeful women rushed upon them,
1367. Stripped the bodies of the wounded,
1368. Women who were raped and beaten,
1369. By the Te-Henu—Siwan soldiers.
     Assembly: By the Te-Henu—Siwan soldiers.

1370. Chemi farmers—Chemi women,
1371. Heard the pleas of Te-Henu—Siwans—
1372. *Oh please spare me—I have children,*
1373. But their pleas were all denied.
     Assembly: But their pleas were all denied.

1374. Taking harvest tools of flint,
1375. Chemi farmers—Chemi women,
1376. Sliced the wounded, slit their bodies,
1377. Te-Henu—Siwans screamed in pain.
     Assembly: Te-Henu—Siwans screamed in pain.

1378. Next came soldiers of the Per-O,
1379. Laughing, smiling, taking tokens,
1380. Slicing hands and slitting tongues,
1381. Slicing ears and parts of men.
     Assembly: Slicing ears and parts of men.

1382. Body trophies for the Man-God,
1383. Mer-En-Ptah the son of the Ramses,
1384. Tongues and hands and parts of men,
1385. Counted by two hundred scribes.
      Assembly: Counted by two hundred scribes.

1386. Per-O raised his flail and crook,
1387. Signaled for a special honor,
1388. Dedication to god Amon—
1389. *Bring me twenty who survived.*
      Assembly: Bring me twenty who survived.

1390. Twenty men their arms bound tightly,
1391. Tethered by their necks were marched,
1392. Unto a place where banners flew—
1393. Bound and led before the King.
      Assembly: Bound and led before the King.

1394. Inside his battle tent sat Per-O,
1395. He the Man-God clothed in splendor,
1396. Dressed in hammered golden raiment,
1397. Crook and flail against his chest.
      Assembly: Crook and flail against his chest.

1398. Though Per-O's spoken words were strange,
1399. The twenty knew their meaning well—
1400. Each wailed for mercy from the Per-O,
1401. But their pleas were all denied.
      Assembly: But their pleas were all denied.

1402. Throughout the lands ruled by the Per-O,
1403. Quickly sped the royal chariots,
1404. From the rear of each was dragged,
1405. A form that once had been a man.
      Assembly: A form that once had been a man.

1406. Ten were Siwans—ten were Te-Henu,
1407. Bound and tied by golden threads,
1408. Dragged the full length of the Black Land,
1409. Until their flesh had disassembled.
       Assembly: Until their flesh had disassembled.

1410. Thus did Per-O son of Ramses,
1411. Show the power of the Chemi,
1412. Subjects cheered and paid him honor,
1413. Cast upon him treasured spices.
       Assembly: Cast upon him treasured spices.

1414. Oh good God-King Son of Ramses,
1415. Oh God-of-Gods how we adore you,
1416. Grant that light from off your brow,
1417. Will ever shine to give us joy.
       Assembly: Will ever shine to give us joy.

1418. There were but few among the Te-Henu,
1419. Fewer still among the Siwans,
1420. Who escaped that desert slaughter,
1421. As one by one they struggled home.
       Assembly: As one by one they struggled home.

1422. God *Zagilie* long had left them,
1423. *Aghourmie* temple lay in ruins,
1424. Prayers once spoken went unanswered,
1425. *Zagilie's* grace had left the valley.
       Assembly: *Zagilie's* grace had left the valley.

1426. Seasons passed then generations,
1427. Years of shame—years of dishonor,
1428. Filled with hatred for the Chemi,
1429. Memories of long ago.
       Assembly: Memories of long ago.

1430. Seasons passed then generations,
1431. Came a time two other peoples,
1432. Meshwesh—Temehu new arrivals,
1433. Came to live within the Siwa.
Assembly: Came to live within the Siwa.

1434. Seasons passed then generations,
1435. All four tribes had merged as one,
1436. Young men clamored for revenge,
1437. But none had felt the pain of battle.
Assembly: But none had felt the pain of battle.

1438. King Libu spoke out in the council:
1439. *We must attack the hated Chemi,*
1440. *Retake the lands that once were ours,*
1441. *Now is the time to plan for war.*
Assembly: Now is the time to plan for war.

1442. Seasons passed then came a time when,
1443. Forges belched new iron weapons,
1444. Vengeance talk grew ever louder,
1445. Blacksmiths hammered iron blades.
Assembly: Blacksmiths hammered iron blades.

1446. Plans were made how to defend,
1447. Against the rush of Chemi chariots,
1448. Hidden pits would be their shield,
1449. Death would be the Per-O's friend.
Assembly: Death would be the Per-O's friend.

1450. Mesher chosen war-time leader,
1451. Stood with Themer, line of Wrmr,
1452. Stood with Tolla, son of Nabis,
1453. Joined with Libu King of Siwa—
Assembly: Joined with Libu King of Siwa—

1454. *Send our spears against the Chemi—*
1455. *Send our arrows straight and true—*
1456. *Send our brave and able warriors—*
1457. *To the Black Land—To the Black Land!*
      Assembly: To the Black Land—To the Black Land!

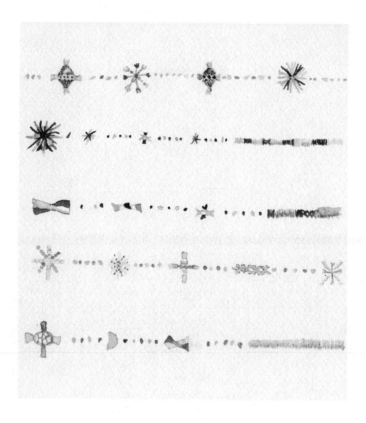

The Fourth Elder rises and recites . . . [Lines 1458-1545].

Marak-ka Ettnin

1458. *Mesher harabeh ra-is,*
1459. *Me'sitah as-kariat sharqet,*
1460. *Wal'lah es-tet ghret es-Chemi,*
1461. *Qat-le we en'hab em-adu.*
   Za'qikla: *Qat-le we en'hab em-adu.*

Battle II

1458. Mesher able war-time leader,
1459. Marched his warriors to the east,
1460. Fired the green fields of the Chemi,
1461. Killed and ravished as before.
   Assembly: Killed and ravished as before.

1462. Each new dawn brought many glories,
1463. Mesher's men were young and strong,
1464. Fighting bravely taking spoils,
1465. Onward marched men from the Siwa.
   Assembly: Onward marched men from the Siwa.

1466. Chemi feared their doom approaching,
1467. Priests sent prayers to Amon-Ra:
1468. *God protect us from the Siwans,*
1469. *Who would take your sacred Black Land.*
   Assembly: Who would take your sacred Black Land.

1470. Fourteen dawns found Siwans camping,
1471. Fourteen dawns since border crossing,
1472. Bodies aching—muscles tired,
1473. Dawn had found them rising slowly.
    Assembly: Dawn had found them rising slowly.

1474. A sense of victory brought an easing,
1475. Of the watchmen's careful scanning,
1476. In the distance rising dust clouds,
1477. Announced the coming of the Chemi.
    Assembly: Announced the coming of the Chemi.

1478. The rising sun god
    Ra-Horakhti,
1479. Caused Siwan eyes to squint
    and turn,
1480. Bright the rising sun Horakhti,
1481. Transformed into the disk of
    Amon.
    Assembly: Transformed into
    the disk of Amon.

Ra-Horakhti blinds the Siwans

1482. From the east there rushed
    upon them,
1483. Sounds of thunder—sounds of
    pounding,
1484. Pulsing foot-beats keeping time to,
1485. Throbbing marching drums of war.
    Assembly: Throbbing marching drums of war.

1486. Across the desert riding westward,
1487. With the light of dawn behind them,
1488. Per-O launched surprise attack,
1489. Charged the sleepy Siwan camp.
    Assembly: Charged the sleepy Siwan camp.

1490. Blinded by the disk of Amon,
1491. Warriors could not aim their spears,
1492. Warriors could not aim their arrows,
1493. None could see the Chemi charging.
    Assembly: None could see the Chemi charging.

1494. Using planks of smoothened wood,
1495. The Chemi spanned the sunken pits,
1496. Crossed into the Siwan camp,
1497. Slaughtered as they had before.
    Assembly: Slaughtered as they had before.

1498. Cried the Siwans—
1499. *Oh god help us—Oh god help us!*
1500. Cried the Te-Henu—
1501. *Oh god help us—Oh god help us!*
    Assembly: Oh god help us—Oh god help us!

1502. Cried the Meshwesh—
1503. *Oh god help us—Oh god help us!*
1504. Cried the Temehu—
1505. *Oh god help us—Oh god help us!*
    Assembly: Oh god help us—Oh god help us!

1506. Onward rushed the troops of Per-O,
1507. From the west the chariots circled,
1508. Sealing off desert retreat—
1509. *Oh god help us—Oh god help us!*
    Assembly: Oh god help us—Oh god help us!

1510. Thousands of the Chemi soldiers,
1511. Raced across the quick spanned pits,
1512. Clouds of battle dust arising,
1513. Clashing blades and shields rang out.
    Assembly: Clashing blades and shields rang out.

1514. Drummers beating—urging onward,
1515. Chemi voices chanting, screaming:
1516. *Give us victory—Give us victory,*
1517. *User-Ma-Re Meri-Amon!*
    Assembly: User-Ma-Re Meri-Amon!

1518. Per-O's chariots blocked retreat,
1519. Then turned towards the fleeing army,
1520. Racing swiftly across the wasteland,
1521. Where no hill could hide the foe.
    Assembly: Where no hill could hide the foe.

1522. Under hooves of beast and blades,
1523. Fell the once proud desert warriors,
1524. All was lost and death was on them,
1525. User-Ma-Re he had conquered.
    Assembly: User-Ma-Re he had conquered.

1526. Oh—the countless brave young Siwans,
1527. Led away and cast in bondage,
1528. Oh—the countless brave young Te-Henu,
1529. Dreams of glory gone astray.
    Assembly: Dreams of glory gone astray.

1530. Oh—the countless brave young Meshwesh,
1531. To ever live as captive slaves,
1532. Oh—the countless brave young Temehu,
1533. Gone forever from their homes.
    Assembly: Gone forever from their homes.

1534. Never more to feel the warmth,
1535. Or pleasure of a loving wife,
1536. Never more to pass the night,
1537. Within the sacred Siwa valley.
    Assembly: Within the sacred Siwa valley.

1538. Ever now to serve the Per-O,
1539. War betrayed them and they wept:
1540. *User-Ma-Re Meri-Amon:*
1541. *Grant us everlasting mercy—*
   Assembly: Grant us everlasting mercy—

1542. *Oh great god—Son of the Sun,*
1543. *Man-god still upon the earth,*
1544. *Grant us everlasting mercy,*
1545. *We are lost—too sad to weep.*
   Assembly: We are lost—too sad to weep.

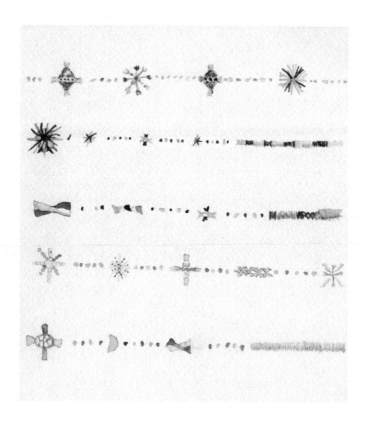

The Fifth Elder rises and recites . . . [Lines 1545-1625].

Ima

1546. *Per-O er-sl't A-Mon kahan-e,*
1547. *T'd ma'sah-ha wadi Siwa,*
1548. *Wuho qe-yas Siwa sarwah,*
1549. *Laz-tum san-nah giz-lah san-nah.*
   Za'qikla: *Laz-tum san-nah giz-lah san-nah.*

Ima

1546. Per-O sent his priest of Amon,
1547. To survey the Siwa valley,
1548. He would measure Siwan bounty,
1549. Set the yearly price of tribute.
   Assembly: Set the yearly price of tribute.

1550. Defeated sons of Marzuk paid,
1551. The price for war against the Chemi,
1552. Food and furs and sacred green stones,
1553. Collected yearly by the victors.
   Assembly: Collected yearly by the victors.

1554. King of Chemi—King of Siwa,
1555. All the valley bowed before him,
1556. User-Ma-Re Meri-Amon,
1557. Siwan gifts for Amon-Ra.
   Assembly: Siwan gifts for Amon-Ra

1558. Amon-Ra wore twisted horns,
1559. Like the ancient Kings of Siwa,
1560. Horns of Amon—horns of *Gurzel,*
1561. Linked together two as one.
     Assembly: Linked together two as one.

1562. Deep inside god Amon's temple,
1563. Built beside the flowing river,
1564. Amon's priests released two birds,
1565. On gentle winds each flew away.
     Assembly: On gentle winds each flew away.

Release of Amon's doves

1566. God's bird of the brightest white,
1567. Like silver in the noon sunlight,
1568. Took to wing and northward flew,
1569. Crossed the boundless sea of *Vanton*—
     Assembly: Crossed the boundless sea of *Vanton*—

1570. She descended at Dodona,
1571. Rested in a grove of trees,
1572. Crinkled leaves sent out a message,
1573. Giving voice to sacred oaks.
     Assembly: Giving voice to sacred oaks.

1574. God's bird of the darkest black,
1575. Like ebony in evening light,
1576. Took to wing above the desert,
1577. Crossed the war-scarred plain of death.
     Assembly: Crossed the war-scarred plain of death.

1578. Onward flew the black bird westward,
1579. Until it reached the Siwa valley.
1580. Overhead she circled twice,
1581. On *Aghourmi's* mount descended.
    Assembly: On *Aghourmi's* mount descended.

1582. Winged messenger from Amon-Ra,
1583. Spoke god's words but none could hear,
1584. Except one girl who wore the disk,
1585. That marked her pure and untouched body.
    Assembly: That marked her pure and untouched body.

1586. Only Ima heard the words,
1587. Spoken by the bird from god,
1588. Only she could hear its message,
1589. Sent from Amon-Ra on high:
    Assembly: Sent from Amon-Ra on high:

1590. *I am He who always will be,*
1591. *I am the One that you once knew,*
1592. *I am the Sun-god of the Chemi,*
1593. *Amon-Ra I speak to you.*
    Assembly: Amon-Ra I speak to you.

1594. *Build anew Aghourmi's temple,*
1595. *Upon the mount where once it stood,*
1596. *I choose you above all maidens,*
1597. *Serve me well and be my bride.*
    Assembly: Serve me well and be my bride.

1598. *You will tend my sacred temple,*
1599. *Keep my altar burning bright,*
1600. *You will tend, prepare my image,*
1601. *Worship me throughout the night.*
    Assembly: Worship me throughout the night.

1602. *Man priests here will number three:*
1603. *One from Siwa, one from Chemi—*
1604. *One from yet a distant time who,*
1605. *Will bring greatness to the valley.*
   Assembly: Will bring greatness to the valley.

1606. *Know this third priest by his shaking,*
1607. *How deep in trance his body falls,*
1608. *He will visit—then depart,*
1609. *But will return and you will know him.*
   Assembly: He will return and you will know him.

1610. *Make the pledge that you will honor,*
1611. *God Zagilie-Amon-Ra,*
1612. *Two as one now as it should be,*
1613. *Merged together two as one.*
   Assembly: Merged together two as one.

Vision of the 3rd Priest

1614. *Faithful Ima heed my message,*
1615. *You are blessed above all others,*
1616. *Wear your disk until the time,*
1617. *The Third Priest needs your care and aid.*
   Assembly: The Third Priest needs your care and aid.

1618. Ima touched the god-bird's feathers,
1619. Felt a joy as none before,
1620. Sins of clan were cleansed forever,
1621. Peace returned within the Siwa.
   Assembly: Peace returned within the Siwa.

1622. The bird of Amon then took flight,
1623. Circled skyward overhead,
1624. Soaring high above *Aghourmi,*
1625. Spinning racing towards the sun.
   Assembly: Spinning racing towards the sun.

The First Elder rises and recites . . . [Lines 1626-1789].

Nep-et

1626. *Per-O sel ke-tub Sen-oui,*
1627. *Sen-oui—qalti zerat-s'ati,*
1628. *Sen-oui—qalti hasi-dat,*
1629. *Sen-oui—qalti hadum-at.*
    Za'qikla: *Sen-oui—qalti hadum-at.*

Nep-et

1626. Per-O sent the scribe Sen-oui,
1627. Sen-oui—ordered planting times,
1628. Sen-oui—ordered harvest times,
1629. Sen-oui—ordered Siwan dress.
    Assembly: Sen-oui—ordered Siwan dress.

1630. Siwa men must wear white clothing,
1631. Draped from men's shoulders to their knees,
1632. Siwa women must wear sunbursts,
1633. Symbols of their ancient god.
    Assembly: Symbols of their ancient god.

1634. Siwan girls must wear their head bands,
1635. Hammered chains and bells of silver,
1636. Siwan boys must shave their heads,
1637. Leaving just one tuft of hair.
    Assembly: Leaving just one tuft of hair.

1638. Sen-oui—ordered gifts to Amon,
1639. Green stones from the Dakrur mines,
1640. Offered to the Chemi's god-King
1641. User-Ma-Re, Meri-Amon.
       Assembly: User-Ma-Re, Meri-Amon.

1642. Men and women of the Siwa,
1643. Came as one, rebuilt the temple,
1644. Ima with her gift of tongues,
1645. Lit the sacred temple fire.
       Assembly: Lit the sacred temple fire.

1646. Ima—she the dark-haired beauty,
1647. Ima—she the bride of god,
1648. Ima—she the pure of heart,
1649. Ima—she the god's own voice.
       Assembly: Ima—she the god's own voice.

1650. One priest from Chemi served her wishes,
1651. Dressed Ima in the finest cloth,
1652. Woven by the Siwan mothers,
1653. Widowed by the Chemi King.
       Assembly: Widowed by the Chemi King.

1654. One priest from Siwa served her wishes,
1655. Daily brought her food and water,
1656. One Chemi priest served all her wishes,
1657. Tended to the temple flame.
       Assembly: Tended to the temple flame.

1658. Ima prayed atop *Aghourmi,*
1659. Stood astride the ancient cleft,
1660. Swirling vapors rose around her,
1661. Clouds from deep inside the earth.
       Assembly: Clouds from deep inside the earth.

1662. Mists from god sent Ima drifting,
1663. Spinning swirling with the stars,
1664. As the words from god enveloped her,
1665. Deep in trance she answered all.
   Assembly: Deep in trance she answered all.

1666. A mighty King from Chefu asked,
1667. *Does danger lurk within my Kingdom?*
1668. Ima's answer served him well,
1669. He found the answer that he sought.
   Assembly: He found the answer that he sought.

1670. Nefer wife of Ramose questioned,
1671. *Will my barren years be ended?*
1672. Ima's answer pleased Ramose,
1673. In one year's time a boy was born.
   Assembly: In one year's time a boy was born.

1674. Tarik King of mighty Byblos,
1675. Learned that death was stalking, waiting,
1676. Ima's answer gave him time to,
1677. Cleanse his life and honor god.
   Assembly: Cleanse his life and honor god.

1678. Visitors from near and far,
1679. People rich and people poor,
1680. Came to hear the words of Ima,
1681. To learn their fate and destiny.
   Assembly: To learn their fate and destiny.

1682. Lapis, gold, and red carnelian,
1683. Amon found such tokens pleasing,
1684. Yet the gifts god treasured most,
1685. Were offered by the poorest pilgrims.
   Assembly: Were offered by the poorest pilgrims.

1686. Pilgrims brought to Siwa knowledge,
1687. New perfected ways of writing,
1688. How to count the passing dawns,
1689. So to gain a sense of time.
   Assembly: So to gain a sense of time.

1690. Priests from distant On and We-Set,
1691. Showed the Siwans how all gods had,
1692. Sprung from Ra, and then from Shu,
1693. Now Nut had born the sacred five.
   Assembly: How Nut had born the sacred five.

1694. Osiris, Isis, Set, and Nepthys,
1695. Elder Horus born to Nut,
1696. Pentad of the Chemi people,
1697. Good and evil born together.
   Assembly: Good and evil born together.

1698. Osiris mated with his sister,
1699. Then was slain by brother Seth,
1700. Osiris he would conquer death,
1701. With Isis sire the falcon Horus.
   Assembly: With Isis sire the falcon Horus.

1702. Horus-Seth then locked in battle,
1703. Uncle-nephew ever clashing,
1704. Battles raged across the heavens,
1705. The Eye of Horus giving light.
   Assembly: The Eye of Horus giving light.

1706. Priests from Chemi taught new ways,
1707. How all dead bodies were revered,
1708. Placed in vats of natron salts,
1709. Prepared within the House of Death.
   Assembly: Prepared within the House of Death.

1710. Seasons passed then generations,
1711. Siwa changed and ever grew,
1712. Now the yoke of Chemi victors,
1713. Lay not heavy as before.
     Assembly: Lay not heavy as before.

1714. Came a stranger to the valley,
1715. Seeking Ima at *Aghourmi*,
1716. The stranger stumbled did not rise,
1717. Two days passed as he lay mute.
     Assembly: Two days passed as he lay mute.

1718. Siwa shamans tried to cure him,
1719. But their ways of healing failed,
1720. Men bore the stranger to the *Mouta,*
1721. Buried him in unmarked grave.
     Assembly: Buried him in unmarked grave.

1722. Six days later those who touched him,
1723. Stumbled, fell, screamed out in pain,
1724. As the sickness spread among them,
1725. Prayers to Amon-Ra all failed.
     Assembly: Prayers to Amon-Ra all failed.

1726. In the darkness of their sorrow,
1727. Out from the desert came a stranger,
1728. A priest of Chemi—aged elder,
1729. He who knew new healing ways.
     Assembly: He who knew new healing ways.

1730. Nep-et the healer mixed three powders,
1731. With the *taut's* cool soothing waters,
1732. Flowing from the sun's own well,
1733. Gave it to the people saying—
     Assembly: Gave it to the people saying—

1734. *Drink from this cup a*
healing mixture,
1735. *When Amon rides his barge at*
night,
1736. *Across the heavens just three*
times,
1737. *The ill in you will leave and*
vanish.
Assembly: The ill in your will
leave and vanish.

Nep-et's healing cup

1738. Nep-et spoke with truth and wisdom,
1739. In three days all sickness vanished,
1740. Once ill people healed and rested,
1741. Shouted loud—*We now are whole.*
Assembly: Shouted loud—We now are whole.

1742. Nep-et came from distant We-Set,
1743. He who saved the lives of many,
1744. Brought to Siwa by their prayers,
1745. Nep-et stood and spoke to all:
Assembly: Nep-et stood and spoke to all.

1746. *My work among you now completed,*
1747. *I have of you a simple wish,*
1748. *Call your young men straight and honest,*
1749. *One will become my healing aide.*
Assembly: One will become my healing aide.

1750. *I will guide him to the Black Land,*
1751. *Into the House of Life to learn,*
1752 *Where he will stay for five long years,*
1753. *Gaining skills in healing arts.*
Assembly: Gaining skills in healing arts.

1754. *But when his days of training end,*
1755. *He will return again to Siwa,*
1756. *He will live and work among you,*
1757 *Sharing gifts and healing skills.*
    Assembly: Sharing gifts and healing arts.

1758. Siwan elders called the young men,
1759. All assembled for selection,
1760. Hunters, farmers, weavers, potters,
1761. Who would accept to follow Nep-et?
    Assembly: Who would accept to follow Nep-et?

1762. Nep-et spoke to all the young men,
1763. How the journey would be long,
1764. How the training in the Black Land,
1765. Would be a test of strength and skill.
    Assembly: Would be a test of strength and skill.

1766. *The House of Life will be your home,*
1767. *Five long years to learn your craft,*
1768. *Five long years away from family,*
1769. *Who would among you follow me?*
    Assembly: Who would among you follow me?

1770. *He who accepts will be alone,*
1771. *Among the Chemi without family,*
1772. *Who among you now will join me,*
1773. *Accept this chance for family honor?*
    Assembly: Accept this chance for family honor?

1774. The Siwan men stood mute before him,
1775. No one spoke, the silence grew,
1776. Then from their midst stepped forth a youth,
1777. Bar-is the son of Khargn spoke—
    Assembly: Bar-is the son of Khargn spoke—

1778. *Nep-et you have come to Siwa,*
1779. *Brought new ways to cure and heal,*
1780. *If you select me on my honor—*
1781. *I will learn and then return.*
    Assembly: I will learn and then return.

1782. Young Bar-is and aged Nep-et,
1783. Joined together for the journey,
1784. Teacher-student clasped their hands,
1785. Bar-is and Nep-et bound as one.
    Assembly: Bar-is and Nep-et bound as one.

1786. A future bright for Marzuk's clan,
1787. Bar-is would become a healer,
1788. But none that day could ever know,
1789. That young Bar-is would not return.
    Assembly: That young Bar-is would not return.

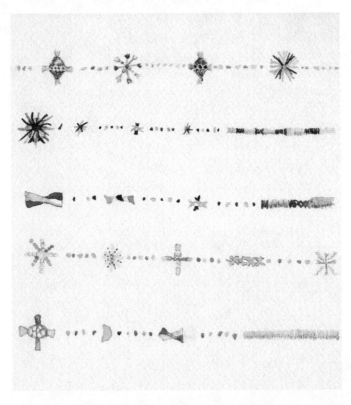

The Second Elder rises and recites . . . [Lines 1790-1977].

Bar-is

1790. Iz-zey bat-al zam-an Tella,
1791. Bar-is et-mast Wa-di Qara,
1792. Nep-et ers-et dym-n Shark-et,
1793. Gamb al-ramb-leh Lak-re-ef.
  Za'qikla: Gamb al-rambleh Lak-re-ef.

Bar-is

1790. Like the distant hero Tella,
1791. Bar-is trekked through Qara Valley,
1792. Nep-et guided ever eastward,
1793. Up to the sands of *Lak-re-ef.*
  Assembly: Up to the sands of *Lak-re-ef.*

1794. At *Lak-re-ef* they took the trail,
1795. Northward of the sinking sands that,
1796. Swallowed careless men and beasts,
1797. Who heeded not the desert dangers.
  Assembly: Who heeded not the desert dangers.

1798. Past the bitter *taut* of *Nebi,*
1799. Where waters seeped through rock and sand,
1800. Taking taste of bitter plants,
1801. So men could not drink their fill.
  Assembly: So men could not drink their fill.

1802. Past the sweet *taut* of *Qat-tara*,
1803. Whose waters clear provided strength,
1804. Two dawns more they reached the *Mag-ra*,
1805. Place of danger, clinging sand.
    Assembly: Place of danger, clinging sand.

1806. Black sand swirling all about them,
1807. Trees of stone upon the dunes,
1808. Nep-et and Bar-is moved quickly,
1809. For to linger meant their doom.
    Assembly: For to linger meant their doom.

1810. Free from the sand but still more desert,
1811. Onward ever towards the east,
1812. Black Land looming in the distance,
1813. Soon they entered Nat-ron valley,
    Assembly: Soon they entered Nat-ron valley.

1814. Here the Chemi mined the na-tron,
1815. To We-Set took the precious salts,
1816. Used by jackal god Anubis,
1817. Lord who ruled the House of Death.
    Assembly: Lord who ruled the House of Death.

1818. Landscapes changed from rock to green,
1819. Fields of plenty all about them,
1820. The lands of Per-O had been reached,
1821. Sacred Black Land of the Chemi.
    Assembly: Sacred Black Land of the Chemi.

1822. Nep-et and Bar-is together,
1823. Reached the broad and flowing river,
1824. Took their place upon a barge,
1825. Sails raised they southward drifted.
    Assembly: Sails raised they southward drifted.

1826. Bar-is looked about in wonder,
1827. Nep-et smiled recalled the days,
1828. When first he ventured from his home,
1829. To find his place within the world.
    Assembly: To find his place within the world.

1830. River barge passed ancient Gi-za,
1831. Sacred plain where Kings were buried,
1832. Under mountains of white stone,
1833. Standing silent by the river.
    Assembly: Standing silent by the river.

1834. Towering tombs of lasting greatness,
1835. Built by hands that loved their Kings,
1836. Pyramids caped with sheets of gold,
1837. Shining white in mid-day sun.
    Assembly: Shining white in mid-day sun.

1838. Near the shore was Men-fer city,
1839. Where the fine white walls once stood,
1840. Now only ruins and temple stones,
1841. Marked this place of former greatness.
    Assembly: Marked this place of former greatness.

1842. Passing Men-fer Nep-et chanted,
1843. Ancient words for long dead spirits,
1844. Hungry, roaming seeking food,
1845. Haunting still this plain of death.
    Assembly: Haunting still this plain of death.

1846. Land of sunset west of Men-fer,
1847. Ruled by Sak-kar god of Death,
1848. Tombs of Chemi Kings and princes,
1849. This Western land, a place of rest.
    Assembly: This Western land, a place of rest.

1850. River barge on southward drifted,
1851. Each new day brought different sights,
1852. Temples, tombs, and rising cities,
1853. Bar-is stared in wonderment.
   Assembly: Bar-is stared in wonderment.

1854. Past great farms and fields of plenty,
1855. Where the Chemi worked and labored,
1856. Cutting grain and threshing *ahmeht*,
1857. Singing joyful songs of harvest.
   Assembly: Singing joyful songs of harvest.

1858. Bar-is watched the girls of Chemi,
1859. Dancing in the harvest circles,
1860. Swaying moving to the drum beast,
1861. Singing with the wailing flutes—
   Assembly: Singing with the wailing flutes—

1862. Songs that praised the gods of harvest,
1863. Bringing hope for coming seasons,
1864. Thanking all the helping gods for,
1865. Yearly sending down the flood.
   Assembly: Yearly sending down the flood.

1866. Two more days of dream-like wonder,
1867. Then came morning through the mist,
1868. Rising skyward temple turrets,
1869. We-Set city now was near.
   Assembly: We-Set city now was near.

1870. Bar-is thanked the elder Nep-et,
1871. For giving chance to serve god Amon,
1872. Both together, youth with elder,
1873. Entered in the House of Life.
   Assembly: Entered in the House of Life.

1874. Lists of healing herbs were many,
1875. Lists of balms and numbing draughts,
1876. Teachers like the elder Nep-et,
1877. Helped the students learn and master.
    Assembly: Helped the students learn and master.

1878. Bar-is learned that Chemi farmers,
1879. Working in their watered fields,
1880. Suffered from the dreaded *aaa*,
1881. Worms that brought an early death.
    Assembly: Worms that brought an early death.

1882. Bar-is learned the healing arts:
1883. How cutting knives were passed through flame,
1884. How slitting veins could heal or kill,
1885. How dim eyesight could be improved.
    Assembly: How dim eyesight could be improved.

House of Life: Chemi medical tools

1886. Seasons passed and then more seasons,
1887. Bar-is grew in healing wisdom,
1888. Teachers praised this youth from Siwa,
1889. For his soothing gentle ways.
    Assembly: For his soothing gentle ways.

1890. How with skill he calmed his patients,
1891. Provided hope and ended fear,
1892. How he touched and eased their pains,
1893. Learning seemed an endless process.
    Assembly: Learning seemed an endless process.

1894. Three years passed and then a fourth,
1895. Tools of healing—herbs and roots,
1896. The cause of pain—new ways to treat,
1897. Learning seemed an endless process.
    Assembly: Learning seemed an endless process.

1898. On the last day of the fifth year,
1899. Healers came throughout the Black Land,
1900. Bar-is stood and faced his teachers,
1901. This the day to test his knowledge.
    Assembly: This the day to test his knowledge.

1902. Soon the questions reached their ending,
1903. Teachers rose, embraced him gladly,
1904. The Master priest then spoke the words:
1905. *Bar-is—now a gifted healer.*
    Assembly: Bar-is—now a gifted healer.

1906. Around his neck for all to see,
1907. The Master placed the bar of
    Sekhmet,
1908. Symbol of the healing arts,
1909. To be worn eternally.
    Assembly: To be worn eternally.

*Baris and Sekhmet's
silver bar*

1910. Nep-et spoke to all assembled,
1911. How Bar-is took up the challenge,
1912. How both left the Siwa valley,
1913. To the sacred Black Land came.
    Assembly: To the sacred Black Land
    came.

1914. Bar-is proud with Sekhmet's symbol,
1915. Offered thanks to all his teachers,
1916. Offered special words to Nep-et,
1917. Words of trust and brotherhood.
    Assembly: Words of trust and brotherhood.

1918. After sunset Nep-et sought him,
1919. Both together crossed the river,
1920. Westward through the fields of grain,
1921. They walked together hand in hand.
    Assembly: They walked together hand in hand.

1922. Temple walls rose in the darkness,
1923. Outlined against the star-lit sky,
1924. A ruined monument of stone,
1925. Where ancient words once carved remained—
    Assembly: Where ancient words once carved remained—

1926. *This the house of User-Ma-Re,*
1927. *King of Kings, Lord of the Reeds,*
1928. *I was He who slew the Siwans,*
1929. *I was He who slew the Te-Henu.*
    Assembly: I was He who slew the Te-Henu.

1930. Upon these towering temple ruins,
1931. Carved by ancient master hands,
1932. Images of war and conquest,
1933. From a time long in the past.
    Assembly: From a time long in the past.

1934. Nep-et and Ba-ris viewed the carvings,
1935. Battles scenes of Siwans-Te-Henu,
1936. Images of chariot warfare,
1937. Chemi fighting desert peoples.
    Assembly: Chemi fighting desert peoples.

1938. Upon these towering temple ruins,
1939. Records of these long-fought battles,
1940. Chemi claimed the Siwans conquered,
1941. Endless lists of yearly tribute.
    Assembly: Endless lists of yearly tribute.

1942. Many years had long since passed,
1943. From the time of User-Ma-Re,
1944. Ancient alters left untended,
1945. No priests to sweep the sand away.
    Assembly: No priests to sweep the sand away.

1946. How these massive temple walls,
1947. Had been transformed by desert sun,
1948. Colors faded, caked with grime,
1949. Mixed with dust of mother earth.
    Assembly: Mixed with dust of mother earth.

1950. User-Ma-Re, once you conquered,
1951. User-Ma-Re, once you ruled,
1952. User-Ma-Re, you were Per-O,
1953. God and man—both one and same.
    Assembly: God and man—both one and same.

1954. Now your temple lies in ruins,
1955. Now today in my far homeland,
1956. We sing tales of Siwan heroes,
1957. Men far greater than yourself.
    Assembly: Men far greater than yourself.

1958. User-Ma-Re still you ride,
1959. Your royal chariot slaying Siwans,
1960. While below you list our tribute,
1961. With names of all our conquered Kings—
    Assembly: With names of all our conquered Kings—

1962. *Wrmer, Mesher, Ferik, Tasher—*
1963. *Felna, Telt, Ferda, Pelo—*
1964. *King of Siwa, young Clearchus,*
1965. *Conquered all in noble combat.*
    Assembly: Conquered all in noble combat.

1966. User-Ma-Re this I tell you,
1967. As you ride in frozen motion,
1968. Our two peoples live in peace,
1969. Siwan—Chemi now are one.
    Assembly: Siwan—Chemi now are one.

1970. User-Ma-Re—we were foes,
1971. User-Ma-Re—King of Kings,
1972. User-Ma-Re—look upon me,
1973. User-Ma-Re—hear my words—
    Assembly: User-Ma-Re—hear my words—

1974. *You once conquered all the world,*
1975. *You once ruled with riches grand,*
1976. *Now today you lie forgotten,*
1977. *In a world of dirt and grime!*
    Assembly: In a world of dirt and grime!

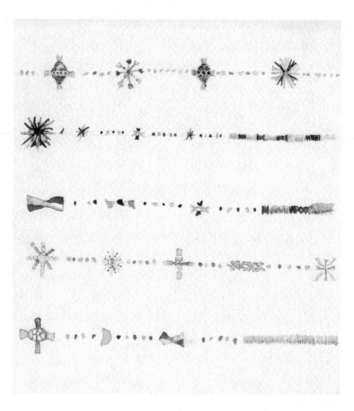

The Third Elder rises and recites . . . [Lines 1978-2049].

Sokkar

1978. *Nep-et ma't ba'd arbat yam,*
1979. *La-kn sahid zhal-kud abna,*
1980. *Rag-zana sa-hetna ely-m,*
1981. *Al-walid kn-t ser-it Ib-nah.*
    Za'qikla: *Al-walid kn-t ser-it Ib-nah.*

Sokkar

1978. Nep-et died just four dawns later,
1979. But happy foster father he,
1980. Gave the gift of healing knowledge,
1981. To a youth he took for son.
    Assembly: To a youth he took for son.

1982. His body stayed for ninety days,
1983. Inside the darkened House of Death,
1984. Amon priests made pure the body,
1985. Wrapped him with the finest linen.
    Assembly: Wrapped him with the finest linen.

1986. All the healing priests assembled,
1987. Aboard the barge of god Anubis,
1988. Silent drifting with the current,
1989. Northward towards the plain of
    Sokkar.
    Assembly: Northward towards the
    plain of Sokkar.

Chemi jackal god of death

1990. Chemi people watched in silence,
1991. Tens of thousands lined the river,
1992. Standing quiet in their mourning,
1993. Offered prayers to healer Nep-et.
Assembly: Offered prayers to healer Nep-et.

1994. Northward through the land of Chem,
1995. Barge and men sailed on in sorrow,
1996. Silent oars dipped through the water,
1997. Until at last their journey ended.
Assembly: Until at last their journey ended.

Nep-et's funeral barge

1998. Where the river broadened wide,
1999. Helmsmen set against the shore.
2000. Across the desert plain of Sokkar,
2001. Sekhmet guided loving priests,
Assembly: Sekhmet guided loving priests.

2002. Up the slanting ramp of Un-Is,
2003. Fallen ruins—broken statues,
2004. Ra sent the sun to light the way,
2005. Songs of praise rose to the sky.
Assembly: Songs of praise rose to the sky.

2006. Past the court of once proud Zo-ser,
2007. Fallen ruins—broken statues,
2008. Goddess of the desert heat,
2009. Sekhmet guided loving priests.
Assembly: Sekhmet guided loving priests.

2010. Past the tomb of Meru-Ka-Ra,
2011. Past the tomb of Ka-Gm-Ni,
2012. Past the tomb of Ank-Ma-Hor,
2013. Three Chemi nobles from the past.
   Assembly: Three Chemi nobles from the past.

2014. Mourners carried Nep-et's coffin,
2015. To the place of highest honor,
2016. Near the crypt where thousands waited,
2017. Near the tomb of god Im-Ho-Tep.
   Assembly: Near the tomb of god Im-Ho-Tep.

2018. Im-Ho-Tep he both god and man,
2019. Foremost of the ancient healers,
2020. Learned healing methods from the gods,
2021. First from Amon then from Sekhmet.
   Assembly: First from Amon then from Sekhmet.

2022. Chemi guardsmen lit the torches,
2023. Priests of Sokkar brought the gifts,
2024. Offerings to god Im-Ho-Tep,
2025. Ibis birds with down-curved bills.
   Assembly: Ibis birds with down-curved bills.

2026. Deep inside the tomb they bore him,
2027. Down the rock-hewn slanting shaft,
2028. They carried Nep-et to his chamber,
2029. Laid to rest near god Im-Ho-Tep.
   Assembly: Laid to rest near god Im-Ho-Tep.

2030. Each then placed a sacred Ibis,
2031. Upon the pile where thousands lay,
2032. Symbolic of the healing arts,
2033. Symbolic of the afterlife.
   Assembly: Symbolic of the afterlife.

2034. Priests performed the ancient rituals,
2035. Nep-et would have proper answers,
2036. He to give the gods when questioned,
2037. Fifty answers for his *ka*.
    Assembly: Fifty answers for his *ka*.

2038. Mourners shared in one last meal,
2039. Near the coffin of their friend,
2040. Upon each wall were healing scenes,
2041. Approved by Nep-et while he lived.
    Assembly: Approved by Nep-et while he lived.

2042. Came the time for mourners leaving,
2043. Back once more into the daylight,
2044. Bar-is now respected healer,
2045. Upward raised his eyes to heaven—
    Assembly: Upward raised his eyes to heaven—

2046. *God Im-Ho-Tep grant me knowledge,*
2047. *God Im-Ho-Tep I implore you—*
2048. *Help me use my skills with honor,*
2049. *Guide me safely to my homeland.*
    Assembly: Guide me safely to my homeland.

The Fourth Elder rises and recites . . . [Lines 2050-2257].

Cam-byses

2050. *Min az-zbad Shar-kya balad,*
2051. *A-geshak min al-bidaq-aswd,*
2052. *Emsti ma-bad dhabla jr-ab,*
2053. *Nass hazimta'kul kud-dam.*
     Za'qikla: *Nass hazimta'kul kud-dam.*

Cambyses

2050. Out from an eastern distant land,
2051. An army of black bearded soldiers,
2052. Marching to the beat of drums,
2053. Defeated all who stood before them.
     Assembly: Defeated all who stood before them.

2054. Closer to the sacred Black Land,
2055. Came the tramping tread of soldiers,
2056. Armor shining in the sunlight,
2057. Ever onward thundered footsteps.
     Assembly: Ever onward thundered footsteps.

2058. Soldiers led by King Cambyses,
2059. Horses, camels, beasts from Persia,
2060. Armor shining in the sunlight,
2061. Ever onward thundered footsteps.
     Assembly: Ever onward thundered footsteps.

2062. A hundred thousand feet were marching,
2063. O'er the Black Land of the Chemi,
2064. King Cambyses dressed in silver,
2065. Looked about and found it pleasing.
    Assembly: Looked about and found it pleasing.

2066. Near the wave-tossed sea of Vanton,
2067. Soldiers frolicked in the breakers,
2068. Men from Persia took their rest then,
2069. Rumbled onward looting, slaying.
    Assembly: Rumbled onward looting, slaying.

2070. Voices from his eager soldiers,
2071. Shouted o'er the war-scorched earth,
2072. Proud their leader, King Cambyses,
2073. Looked about and found it pleasing,
    Assembly: Looked about and found it pleasing.

2074. *Lead us! O Cambyses lead us!*
2075. *Onward to the flowing river,*
2076. *To the Black Land—to the Black Land,*
2077. *We will destroy the land of Chem!*
    Assembly: They will destroy the land of Chem!

2078. *Lead us! Oh, Cambyses, lead us!*
2079. *We will drink the blood of Per-O,*
2080. *It is written oh, Cambyses,*
2081. *You will seize the double crown!*
    Assembly: You will seize the double crown.

2082. The cloak of Persian darkness spread,
2083. Across the ancient land of Chem,
2084. The land that once saw glory days,
2085. Could not halt the Persian hoard.
    Assembly: Could not halt the Persian hoard.

2086. Near the ancient city Men-Fer,
2087. Cambyses slew the sacred Apis,
2088. Thrust his sword into its belly,
2089. Cambyses laughed as Apis died.
    Assembly: Cambyses laughed as Apis died.

2090. Oh, the mournful priests at Men-Fer,
2091. Chanted o'er their still warm bull-god,
2092. Pleaded for a time of reckoning,
2093. Soon to come—oh, soon to come.
    Assembly: Soon to come—oh, soon to come.

2094. King Cambyses conquered We-Set,
2095. Tore down Amon's Kar-Nak temple,
2096. Seized the throne and double crown,
2097. Symbols of the Per-O's rule.
    Assembly: Symbols of the Per-O's rule.

2098. King Cambyses ruled the Black Land,
2099. His reign sent fear throughout the nation,
2100. Those who spoke against Cambyses,
2101. Died—impaled on Persian pikes.
    Assembly: Died—impaled on Persian pikes.

2102. Standing near the western cliffs,
2103. The largest statue in the world,
2104. Cambyses thought the statue mocking,
2105. Ordered smashed upon the ground.
    Assembly: Ordered smashed upon the ground.

2106. Cambyses traveled through the Black Land,
2107. Erased the names of Chemi Kings,
2108. Destroyed the fine-carved words of Amon,
2109. *I am god Cambyses claimed.*
    Assembly: I am god Cambyses claimed.

2110. Cries of anguish from the Chemi,
2111. Fell on covered Persian ears,
2112. Priests of Amon at his temple,
2113. All were slain but one named Ai—
    Assembly: All were slain but one named Ai—

2114. Under blades of Persian torture,
2115. Priests revealed the hidden treasure,
2116. Wherein the ark of Amon lay,
2117. Filled with gifts fit for the god.
    Assembly: Filled with gifts fit for the god.

2118. Cambyses smashed the ark of cedar,
2119. Desecrated god's own treasure,
2120. Stole the bars of gold and silver,
2121. Stones that shone like greenish eyes.
    Assembly: Stones that shone like greenish eyes.

2122. Oh—the green stones—greatest treasure,
2123. Their mines and sources must be found,
2124. One mine was distant to the south,
2125. Another was within the Siwa.
    Assembly: Another was within the Siwa.

2126. What of the priest who sold his soul,
2127. Who told the Persians of the stones?
2128. He who lived while others died,
2129. Ai had dishonored god—
    Assembly: Ai had dishonored god—

2130. *Come forward priest for your reward . . .*
2131. Ai knelt in fear and weakness:
2132. *Spare my life oh King Cambyses,*
2133. *I gave you knowledge of the mines.*
    Assembly: I gave you knowledge of the mines.

2134. *Of course, my priest,* the mad King smiled,
2135. *Come forward priest for your reward . . .*
2136. *Oh, spare my life good King Cambyses,*
2137. *I have served you well my King.*
    Assembly: I have served you well my King.

2138. Ai groveled on the ground,
2139. He pleaded for a longer life,
2140. Cambyses signaled with his hand—
2141. With one quick slash—and it was done.
    Assembly: With one quick slash—and it was done.

2142. Cambyses rose and gave new orders:
2143. *Select our best troops strong and able,*
2144. *Thirty thousand soldiers ready,*
2145. *Onward we shall march to Siwa.*
    Assembly: Onward we shall march to Siwa.

2146. *Prepare water, food, and horses,*
2147. *We will march across the wasteland,*
2148. *Heat and thirst will be companions,*
2149. *We may need a healing priest.*
    Assembly: We may need a healing priest.

2150. Cambyses ordered priests of Sekhmet,
2151. Each to come and stand before him,
2152. One by one each priest inspected,
2153. One by one each sent away,
    Assembly: One by one each sent away.

2154. Cambyses sought the strongest healer,
2155. Older priests he sent away.
2156. Cambyses searched but for the strongest,
2157. Then stood Bar-is before the King.
    Assembly: Then stood Bar-is before the King.

2158. *You will tend to healing duties,*
2159. *Restore my soldiers who may falter,*
2160. *From the heat of desert march,*
2161. *Use your knowledge for our good.*
    Assembly: Use your knowledge for our good.

2162. In the month of *Ka-hr-ka* they,
2163. Crossed the silent flowing river,
2164. Passed the tombs cut into rock,
2165. Climbed and reached the valley rim.
    Assembly: Climbed and reached the valley rim.

2166. Such a force could not move quickly,
2167. The army trekked for seven days,
2168. Until they reached the Blessed Isles,
2169. Filled with *tauts* and trees of fruit.
    Assembly: Filled with *tauts* and trees of fruit.

Persian troops depart for the Siwa

2170. Weary Persian soldiers rested,
2171. Bodies tired from desert march,
2172. Time to rest, repair their bodies,
2173. Drinking water from the *tauts.*
    Assembly: Drinking water from the *tauts.*

2174. At sunset Bar-is walked among them,
2175. Past the campfires filled with laughter,
2176. Heard the drunken plans of looting,
2177. Temple treasures from the Siwa.
    Assembly: Temple treasure from the Siwa.

2178. Heard the plan to burn Aghourmi,
2179. Kill the priestess seer, Ima,
2180. Gather all the sacred green stones,
2181. Taken from the Siwan mines.
    Assembly: Taken from the Siwan mines.

2182. Bar-is knew what he must do,
2183. Bar-is knew Cambyses lied,
2184. He must prevent this evil plan,
2185. Stop the soldiers from their march.
    Assembly: Stop the soldiers from their march.

2186. Bar-is went against his training,
2187. With poison planned to kill the Persians,
2188. He would mix death with their food,
2189. In this way save Siwa valley.
    Assembly: In this way save Siwa valley.

2190. As Bar-is mixed the deadly drugs,
2191. Persian spies observed his actions,
2192. They bound Bar-is, slit his belly,
2193. Broke his legs, his arms, and hands.
    Assembly: Broke his legs, his arms, and hands.

2194. Bar-is was dragged to Daxis' tent,
2195. He the leader of the Persians,
2196. There the soldiers did more evil,
2197. Bar-is was blinded, tongue removed!
    Assembly: Bar-is was blinded, tongue removed!

2198. Bar-is of Siwa left his homeland,
2199. Bar-is became a healing priest,
2200. Bar-is of Siwa passed successful,
2201. From the Chemi House of Life.
    Assembly: From the Chemi House of Life.

2202. Bar-is who learned to heal and love,
2203. Who longed again to see his homeland,
2204. No longer felt the cuts of Daxis,
2205. Death embraced him dark and cold.
    Assembly: Death embraced him dark and cold.

2206. Down upon this scene of torture,
2207. Amon's sacred dove was watching,
2208. Its beating wings gave out no sound,
2209. As swift it flew a northern course.
  Assembly: As swift it flew a northern course.

2210. Across the desert dark with danger,
2211. Amon's dove sped to the Siwa,
2212. Landed at *Aghourmi's* temple,
2213. Told Ima of coming danger.
  Assembly: Told Ima of coming danger.

2214. Siwans offered up their prayers,
2215. *Amon-Ra protect our valley,*
2216. Siwans offered up their prayers,
2217. *God Zagilie save our valley.*
  Assembly: God Zagilie save our valley.

2218. Northward from the Blessed Islands,
2219. Daxis marched the Persian soldiers:
2220. *Onward soldiers we must hasten,*
2221. *Through these endless dunes of sand.*
  Assembly: Through these endless dunes of sand.

2222. Two more dawns the Persians marched,
2223. Eager for to take their spoils,
2224. Greed engulfed them, flamed their voices,
2225. *We will take the green-stone treasure.*
  Assembly: We will take the green-stone treasure.

2226. Men and women at the Siwa,
2227. Offered prayers to god *Zagilie,*
2228. *Save us from the Persian soldiers,*
2229. *Who would take your temple from us.*
  Assembly: Who would take your temple from us.

2230. Men and women at the Siwa,
2231. Offered prayers to Amon-Ra,
2232. *Save us from the Persian soldiers,*
2233. *Who would take your temple from us.*
    Assembly: Who would take your temple from us.

2234. Siwan gods and gods of Chemi,
2235. Heard the pleas upon the breeze,
2236. Amon-Ra and god *Zagilie,*
2237. Sent the southern winds to rise—
    Assembly: Sent the southern winds to rise—

2238. Across the desert growing stronger,
2239. Blowing finest choking dust,
2240. Stronger grew the sandy winds,
2241. Sapping strength from Persian soldiers.
    Assembly: Sapping strength from Persian soldiers.

2242. Day-time appeared as deepest night,
2243. Wind-born sand raged all about them,
2244. The soldiers felt the touch of fear—
2245. The sword of doubt had been unleashed.
    Assembly: The sword of doubt had been unleashed.

2246. Shrill the wind increased its tempo,
2247. Horses screamed in fearful terror,
2248. Chests of water fell and burst,
2249. Spilling contents on the earth.
    Assembly: Spilling contents on the earth.

2250. Thirst-parched men cried out for water,
2251. Soldiers blinded by the sandstorm,
2252. One by one their bodies fell,
2253. Upon the wind-tossed dunes of sand.
Assembly: Upon the wind-tossed dunes of sand.

Death by sandstorm

2254. Thirty thousand Persians perished,
2255. Within this violent storm of sand,
2256. And still today there is no mark,
2257. To show that they had ever lived.
Assembly: To show that they had ever lived.

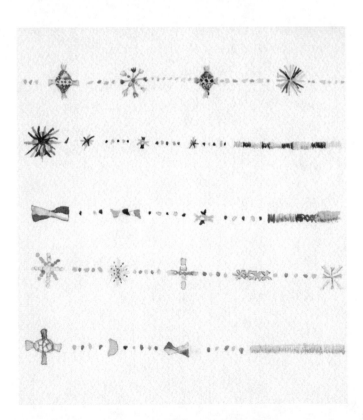

The Fifth Elder rises and recites . . . [Lines 2258-2454].

Is-Kander

2258. *El-at Siwa, el-at Chemi,*
2259. *Esmat ra'ghtkl-wat al-Siwat,*
2260. *Amon-Ra weh Ell Zagilie,*
2261. *Ta-wsh 'kul a-nass al-Siwa.*
     Za'qikla: *Ta-wsh 'kul a-nass al-Siwa.*

Iskander

2258. Siwan gods and gods of Chemi,
2259. Heard the heart-felt Siwan pleas,
2260. Amon-Ra and god *Zagilie,*
2261. Saved the Siwa and the people.
     Assembly: Saved the Siwa and the people.

2262. From the distant lands of earth,
2263. Pilgrims came to learn their future,
2264. Many sought a glimpse of glory,
2265. Others questioned length of life.
     Assembly: Others questioned length of life.

2266. Seasons passed and then more seasons,
2267. Peace now reigned throughout the Siwa,
2268. Per-O ruled again the Chemi,
2269. Hated Persians were destroyed.
     Assembly: Hated Persians were destroyed.

2270. But with the waning years of Per-O,
2271. The ancient empire would be lost,
2272. Chemi Black Land now in twilight,
2273. Chemi Black Land weak and old.
    Assembly: Chemi Black Land weak and old.

2274. Once again out from the East,
2275. Arose new pounding drums of war,
2276. A second distant Persian King,
2277. Desired to rule the ancient Black Land.
    Assembly: Desired to rule the ancient Black Land.

2278. But far away and to the north,
2279. A worthy ruler wise and just,
2280. Born in the ancient city Pella,
2281. Son of Philip named Is-Kander—
    Assembly: Son of Philip named Is-Kander—

2282. With his army bold and strong he,
2283. Freed all peoples from oppression,
2284. Left his men to rule in justice,
2285. Nations praised his youth and name.
    Assembly: Nations praised his youth and name.

2286. In the fabled land of Midas,
2287. Is-Kander solved the ancient puzzle,
2288. With his sword he sliced the knot,
2289. That could not be untied by man.
    Assembly: That could not be untied by man.

2290. By this deed he gained protection,
2291. From the ever present gods,
2292. He was promised at Gordium,
2293. All the world would kneel before him.
    Assembly: All the world would kneel before him.

2294. Is-Kander's men at Issus stood,
2295. While Persian, Darius, fled in fear,
2296. Took to a chariot, crossed the desert,
2297. Abandoned dark-eyed wife and mother.
   Assembly: Abandoned dark-eyed wife and mother.

2298. Fair and blue-eyed King Is-Kander,
2299. Found the Persian women frightened,
2300. Treated them with highest honor,
2301. Returned them safely to their home.
   Assembly: Returned them safely to their home.

2302. Is-Kander, he of youthful vigor,
2303. Marched his troops along the sea,
2304. He would free the land of Chemi,
2305. From the threat of Persian conquest.
   Assembly: From the threat of Persian conquest.

2306. Black Land priests received him gladly,
2307. Gave him glory—gave him honor,
2308. In the southern city We-Set,
2309. Is-Kander gained the double crown.
   Assembly: Is-Kander gained the double crown.

2310. He Is-Kander—son of Phillip,
2211. Twenty eight his years of life,
2312. Now he ruled the land of Chemi,
2313. Ancient Black Land of the Per-O.
   Assembly: Ancient Black Land of the Per-O.

2314. *Oh Is-Kander son of Amon,*
2315. *Share with us of your lasting glory,*
2316. *Oh Is-Kander son of Amon,*
2317. *Share with us your truth and wisdom.*
   Assembly: Share with us your truth and wisdom.

2318. Is-Kander puzzled by such words,
2319. Caused his mind to ever wonder,
2320. Was he sired by man or god?
2321. How could he learn his father's name?
  Assembly: How could he learn his father's name?

2322. Night-time dreams brought shaking tremors,
2323. Caused his body to transform,
2324. Twisting wreathing on the ground,
2325. Is-Kander fell into a trance.
  Assembly: Is-Kander fell into a trance.

2326. Priests of We-Set in the morning,
2327. Told Is-Kander of the Siwa,
2328. Urged the god-King he must go,
2329. Seek Amon's words from priestess Ima.
  Assembly: Seek Amon's words from priestess Ima.

2330. Is-Kander sailed by northern barge,
2331. Along the river's western branch,
2332. Five dawns saw his troops assemble,
2333. Set their camp along the sea.
  Assembly: Set their camp along the sea.

2334. Just beyond the shore of *Vanton,*
2335. An island offered ship protection,
2336. Is-Kander saw this place of promise,
2337. Gave the order: build a city—
  Assembly: Gave the order: build a city—

2338. Bring stone masons:—build a city,
2339. One to last throughout the ages,
2340. A city that will bear my name,
2341. A place for all to come and learn.
  Assembly: A place for all to come and learn.

2342. Order given—time to march,
2343. Westward towards the setting sun,
2344. In the time of seven days,
2345. They reached the town, Amon-ium.
   Assembly: They reached the town, Amon-ium.

2346. Here the priests from far Cyrene,
2347. Offered gifts of gold and silver,
2348. *Oh Is-Kander son of god,*
2349. *We have waited for your coming.*
   Assembly: We have waited for your coming.

2350. Southward 'cross the desert marching,
2351. Is-Kander and his troops from Pella,
2352. Southward towards the valley Siwa,
2353. Marching through the heat of day.
   Assembly: Marching through the heat of day.

2354. In time they took a wrong direction,
2355. Soldiers suffered thirst and heat,
2356. Then appeared a ram from nowhere,
2357. Amon's ram then led them southward.
   Assembly: Amon's ram then led them southward.

2358. Khumn, the ram god sent by Amon,
2359. Saved Is-Kander and his soldiers,
2360. Southward ever southward marching,
2361. Until they reached the valley Siwa.
   Assembly: Until they reached the valley Siwa.

2362. Light of dusk shown like pure gold,
2363. Amon's ram had led them safely,
2364. Through the desert to the Siwa,
2365. Now the people came to greet him.
   Assembly: Now the people came to greet him.

2366. He the ruler of the Chemi,
2367. Is-Kander, he the distant King,
2368. He who honors all the peoples,
2369. Bringing peace uniting men.
   Assembly: Bringing peace uniting men.

2370. Is-Kander sought the priestess Ima,
2371. She advanced with outstretched arms,
2372. They together climbed *Aghourmi*,
2373. Entered Amon's sacred temple.
   Assembly: Entered Amon's sacred temple.

2374. Once inside the spirit seized him,
2375. Is-Kander trembled, slumped and fell,
2376. Upon the floor of Amon's temple,
2377. As the light of god shown down.
   Assembly: As the light of god shown down.

2378. Ima rode the chair of vision,
2379. Sitting o'er the gaping fissure,
2380. Vapors from the earth enveloped her,
2381. Ima fell into a trance.
   Assembly: Ima fell into a trance.

2382. Through the swirling mists god spoke,
2383. Of early times, Is-Kander's birth,
2384. How that he was son of God,
2385. Yet at same time son of man.
   Assembly: Yet at same time son of man.

2386. Ima chanted Amon's words,
2387. Vapors swirling all about her,
2388. Is-Kander's body twisting turning,
2389. Amon's words poured gently o'er them.
   Assembly: Amon's words poured gently o'er them.

2390. Ima stripped his dusty armor,
2391. Covered with the grime of march,
2392. Bathed his fevered troubled body,
2393. With cool waters from the *taut*.
    Assembly: With cool waters from the *taut*.

2394. Ima tended to Is-Kander,
2395. Embraced him through his shaking time,
2396. Ima pressed her warmth against him,
2397. Both together merged as one.
    Assembly: Both together merged as one.

2398. Two days passed they stayed inside,
2399. The temple high above *Aghourmi*,
2400. Is-Kander found what he had sought,
2401. But god Amon commanded silence.
    Assembly: But god Amon commanded silence.

2402. *Never speak my words revealed,*
2403. *You are god but live as man,*
2404. *Never speak what I have told you,*
2405. *I alone command your fate.*
    Assembly: I alone command your fate.

2406. Deep inside *Aghourmi's* temple,
2407. Ima tended Amon's image,
2408. She the sacred bride of god,
2409. Knew *Zagilie's* prophecy—
    Assembly: Knew *Zagilie's* prophecy—

2410. *He who trembled would take rest,*
2411. *Stay among them but would leave,*
2412. *He who trembled—he the Third Priest,*
2413. *Would return again to Siwa.*
    Assembly: Would return again to Siwa.

2414. Is-Kander called the elders to him,
2415. Spoke of justice for all people,
2416. Held the hand of priestess Ima,
2417. Spoke to her—he must now leave.
    Assembly: Spoke to her—he must now leave.

2418. Eastward marched the young Is-Kander,
2419. Like Tella ancient Siwan King,
2420. He passed through Qara then through Mag-rah,
2421. Like the Siwan hero Bar-is.
    Assembly: Like the Siwan hero Bar-is.

2422. Great his many splendid conquests,
2423. Is-Kander moved on ever eastward,
2424. He would form the greatest empire,
2425. That the world would ever know.
    Assembly: That the world would ever know.

2426. One that stretched from distant homeland,
2427. Far across the sea of *Vanton,*
2428. Eastward-westward grew his conquests,
2429. Is-Kander he now ruled the world.
    Assembly: Is-Kander he now ruled the world.

2430. But three years later as predicted,
2431. Is-Kander fell, but not by sword,
2432. At Babylon he died of fever,
2433. Never more to walk the earth.
    Assembly: Never more to walk the earth.

2434. At Babylon Is-Kander's body,
2435. Lay waiting for the priests of Chem,
2436. Back they bore him to the Black Land,
2437. Within a coffin honey filled.
    Assembly: Within a coffin honey filled.

2438. God Anubis gave protection,
2439. Chemi priests prepared his body,
2440. One said he must lie in honor,
2441. Within his proud white seaside city—
   Assembly: Within his proud white seaside city—

2442. Inside a chest of clearest glass,
2443. Priests placed the body of Is-Kander,
2444. At the crossing of two roads,
2445. Inside a tomb where all could see.
   Assembly: Inside a tomb where all could see.

Iskander's body inside glass coffin

2446. Through the night the soldier guards,
2447. Re-told stories of their battles,
2448. Drank white wine with taste of resin,
2449. Feasting as the King lay near.
   Assembly: Feasting as the King lay near.

2450. Morning dawned with light and stillness
2451. Priests approached the tomb of glass,
2452. One last look at King Is-Kander—
2453. God protect us: he has vanished—!
   Assembly: God protect us: he has vanished—!

Al-Kahana Thalthe

2454. *Min al-wadi badid Siwa,*
2455. *Raggat zam-bin fa-gr gadid,*
2456. *Zam-bin ig-rid tal-tet az-zim,*
2457. *Min af-fet beit-um nas-Marzuk.*
   Za'qikla: *Min af-fet beit-um nas-Marzuk.*

The Third Priest

2454. In the distant valley Siwa,
2455. Echoed sounds of morning dawn,
2456. Sounds of coming greatness flowed,
2457. Within the blood of Marzuk's clan.
   Assembly: Within the blood of Marzuk's clan.

2458. Loud the chanting—rising falling,
2459. As the earth rose up and trembled,
2460. Ima offered hymns of glory,
2461. All waited for the coming greatness.
   Assembly: All waited for the coming greatness.

*Ima prays for return of
the Third Priest*

169

2462. From *Aghourmi's* mountain temple,
2463. Came the words god sent to Ima—
2464. *He has returned—he has returned!*
2465. And the Third Priest dwelt among them.
Assembly: *Del-wat Imi Talta saket . . .*

Del-wat Imi Talta saket:
[Third Priest has returned]

*** [END]

The following phrase was shouted and repeated six times by those assembled:

Del-wat Imi Talta saket . . . Del-wat Imi Talta saket.

Del-wat Imi Talta saket . . . Del-wat Imi Talta saket.

Del-wat Imi Talta saket . . . Del-wat Imi Talta saket.

[And the Third Priest dwelt among them . . . And the Third Priest dwelt among them].

[And the Third Priest dwelt among them . . . And the Third Priest dwelt among them].

[And the Third Priest dwelt among them . . . And the Third Priest dwelt among them].

PART 3

After Notes

Climax: Unveiling and Presentation of the Relic

The recitation was over. Sunrise pierced the morning mist hovering over the oasis and burst forth with blazing fire illuminating the jagged skyline of the ruined Aghourmi temple. With the final verses of *The Song of Siwa* finished, we stood—mesmerized—awaiting the *mulid* climax!

The first elder remained standing as the others rose and took their places beside him. The first elder retired to the mountain temple while we below waited in hushed silence. After about twenty minutes, he reemerged from the ruins holding a small cedar chest—a box girded with silver hasps and decorated on the lid with a geometric Macedonian star. The first elder held the chest high above his head for all of us to see. Next, the four remaining elders slowly climbed the stone steps and joined him atop Aghourmi. We below cried out in anticipation as the first elder opened the chest. He motioned and signaled to a drummer who initiated a rhythmic cadence—soft initially, then louder—as we below watching shouted in unison:

ik-ful [open] . . .

ik-ful [open] . . .

ik-ful [open] . . .

ik-ful [open] . . .

Responding, the first elder reached inside the chest and removed a purple cloth wrapped around a concealed item. He removed the protective cloth and passed the object to each of the elders in turn for their inspection and confirmation. After each had inspected the relic the fifth elder returned it to the first elder with respect and honor. We in the gathered assembly waited in anticipation . . . responding to our cries the first elder held the relic high above his head for all to see. Standing at the base of Aghourmi, with the ancient temple towering over us, we remained in hushed silence as we gazed upon—an ancient copper knife!

The first elder pointed to the master drummer who began a nine-beat rhythmic cadence as we chanted aloud the following names in sequence:

Marzuk, Tella, Baris, Is-Kander . . .

Marzuk, Tella, Baris, Is-Kander . . .

Marzuk, Tella, Baris, Is-Kander . . .

Marzuk, Tella, Baris, Is-Kander . . .

The first elder took the copper knife and lifted it high above his head as the sun's disk emerged fully above the eastern horizon. He blessed all of us attending and with reverence re-wrapped the knife within its protective purple cloth and replaced the bundle inside the ancient cedar chest—to be opened and displayed during the next *mulid* on the fifteenth day, fifteen years in the future.

The first elder concluded the ceremony by reciting the traditional ancient Siwan benediction:

Is-Kander Humah;
Is-Kander humah ma-nahi, al-beit Marzuk.

Iskander Protector;
Iskander protect us all, we the lineage of Marzuk.

* * *

Coda

The events described here ended shortly after dawn on the 16th of April, 1965, as the sun emerged behind the ruined spires of the temple on Aghourmi Mountain. After the events concluded I looked about and found myself among friends. I certainly counted myself among the fortunate. I walked as part of a group towards the government rest house and found myself among hundreds of men and women bonded by this astonishing experience. Along the way I linked arms with new Siwan and Qaran friends who continued to comment and marvel at what we had experienced together. No longer was I a foreigner; the experience had united us. My hand was grasped in friendship by dozens who cried out to me as we walked . . .

> *Qalem kull eh-wahid—*
> *Qalem kull eh-wahid fil balidak—*
> *Qalem kull eh-wahid fil balidak—ma'h shuft weh ma'h esmat—*

> *Tell everyone—*
> *Tell everyone in your country—*
> *Tell everyone in your country what you have seen and heard.*

Through preparation of this document I have honored their requests . . .

A week later in the early morning I trekked to the central square where I sat with Siwan friends and conversed over cups of tea. Then it came time to leave . . . I boarded the bus for the long difficult ride north to Mersa Matruh on the coast. But on this northward journey across the bleak and seemingly endless Western Desert of Egypt—where long ago Siwans and Chemi once clashed in chariot warfare—where Alexander the Great once had trekked southward towards Siwa—I carried with me memories of events to last a lifetime.

*　　*　　*

On November 2nd 2012, I received notice that the next *mulid* would be celebrated in the year 2025, with month and date still to be determined. At that time I will be 87 years old. While today I am in good health, only God knows if I will be able to attend. I replied to the notice and sent word to the Aghourmi elders responding to their kind invitation, saying that I would make every attempt to join them—*in-sha Allah*—if God permits. And as I write these concluding words, I plan to attend but between now and then, should bodily infirmities prevent my journey, the Aghourmi elders will know that my heart and spirit will participate—for my thoughts are with them always.

Louis Grivetti
Davis, California
2013

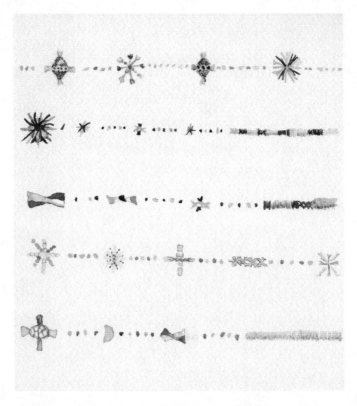

Appendices

Appendix A

The Song of Siwa: Synopsis and Thematic Development

The following synopsis is included here to demonstrate thematic flow and development. A full study and analysis of the 21 distinct sub-topics with potential parallels with other North African and Middle Eastern epics await further academic consideration.

As I attended the festival only once, the oral version recorded and transcribed here may or may not be consistent with earlier or subsequent presentations. The present version of *The Song of Siwa* consists of 21 distinct components. The longest chanted segment (Manhood) contains 211 lines; the shortest (The Third Priest) is represented by only 11. All together this version of the epic has 2465 lines. There is nothing magical or mathematically significant about the number 2465; given that the event was an oral recitation there may be additional verses that accidentally could have been omitted during the presentation.

The chanted words flowing from the elders to those of us in the audience were captivating. As I listened to the drums and words that evening logical questions flowed through my mind:

What master story-teller originally conceived the saga?

Who assumed the responsibility to assemble the verses in their present sequence—a vast time period from remote antiquity to the era of Alexander the Great?

If originally penned as a written document could the manuscript have been lost in the great fire that consumed the Library at Alexandria?

Could it have been that after the fire a group of ancient scholars developed the oral tradition that served as the foundation for the present work?

Could there be earlier written versions? If so, what variants of the epic might exist preserved in still undiscovered localities?

Are there similar or parallel festivals (*mulids*) celebrated by other Berber-speaking groups in the al-Haggar, Air, or Tibesti regions that have not been documented?

Is it possible that different versions of The Song of Siwa, the epic of Marzuk and his clan, continue on today in these geographical areas as well?

In bringing this work to its present form, I find it astonishing that still today in the 21st century at this remote oasis in the Western Desert of Egypt the male elders continue to wear "togas" in the Greek tradition. There is something wonderful, too, about the custom still practiced today where young Siwan girls prior to their marriage proudly wear their silver virginity disks. But most of all is it not remarkable that in south-central Libya, there is an oasis that still today maintains the name Marzuk? And also fascinating is the fact that today at Kharga oasis in the Western Desert of modern Egypt, there is a small settlement and spring named Bar-is!

Song of Siwa: Chapter Summaries . . .

Beginning (lines 1-65).

Ethereal description of the hidden valley Siwa;

Marzuk and his clan of Ice-Age hunters seek protection from environmental changes;

Marzuk senses approaching ice will doom his people;

Marzuk leads his clan to new caves near the Sea of Vanton;

Pine-tree spirits speak to Marzuk that death awaits if his clan remains by the sea;

Marzuk completes construction of pine-log rafts to cross the Sea of Vanton;

Clan members debate whether or not to trust and follow Marzuk;

Marzuk and followers depart while the others remain behind;

Wind and waves batter the rafts as they cross the Sea of Vanton;

Weakest clan members are swept overboard and disappear;

Survivors reach the shore of what is now North Africa;

Clan members who remained behind perish under layers of grinding glacial ice;

The hidden valley Siwa awaits its first human occupants.

Eastward (lines 66-149).

The North African coastal lands breed illness and danger among Marzuk's clan;

The clan splits: Marzuk leads his faction southward while others remain along the coast;

The clan passes through high mountains into the vast Sahara region;

Illness and danger continue to plague Marzuk's clan during their journey;

Many clansmen lose hope and begin to murmur;

God Zaghilie sends messenger bird and a life-saving spring is revealed;

Gosla, Marzuk's mate, promises to erect a temple to god Zaghilie at journey's end;

Feathers from the messenger bird float earth-ward as symbols of hope and safety;

Renewed in spirit Marzuk's clan continue their eastward trek.

Promise (lines 150-277).

The long march continues as clan members fear god-sent promise was only a vision;

Advance scouts cross the Great Sand Sea and view the Siwa for the first time;

Scouts report that the Siwa is filled with wild game and springs of clear water;

Marzuk's clan reaches the Siwa and establishes their settlement near Aghourmi hill;

Clan members erect Zaghili's temple atop Aghourmi thus fulfilling Gosla's promise;

Clan members offer sacred green stones as ritual offerings to god Zaghili;

Zaghili descends and promises clan protection if his rules are followed;

Rules for clan behavior, personal dress, and body ornamentation are identified;

Mothers must display sunburst designs on their dress symbolic of Zaghili's feathers;

Fathers must prepare silver disks for virgin daughters to wear;

Daughters must wear their disks until marriage, then pass them to younger sisters;

Sons must honor their fathers and mothers;

Zaghili promises Gosla the line of Marzuk will flourish if his requirements are followed;

Zaghili requires clan leaders to wear the horns of Gurzel [ram-god] as a symbol of power;

Zaghili specifies rules for maintaining Aghourmi's temple flame;

Zaghili promises that if rules are kept Marzuk's line will not experience strife;

Zaghili blocks the sun's light;

The clan agrees to honor Zaghili's requirements and sunlight returns to the Siwa;

The grace of Zaghili now resides within the line of Marzuk.

Manhood (lines 278-489).

Relation on clan hunting and tracking skills;

Relation on the valor and strength of Marzuk;

Gosla becomes pregnant;

Relation on clan birth practices;

Gosla delivers twins as birth attendants watch in fear;

Gosla rejects clan tradition that requires the death of one twin;

Relation on the growth and maturation of the twins Zel and Zechen;

Zel and Zechen mature and undergo initiation, scarification rituals, and fasting;

Each twin required to prepare spear points, track, and kill a *farna* [leopard];

Zechen killed by a *farna* during his hunting initiation;

Zel kills a *farna*, honors his father, and becomes a man.

Death (lines 490-573).

Marzuk anguishes over the death of his son Zechen;

Glim's cautionary words uttered at the birthing time of the twins are recalled;

Relation on the aging of Marzuk and Gosla;

Relation on Gosla's illness and impending death;

Death of Gosla;

Relation on clan burial and mourning rituals;

Family and mourners bury Gosla at the Mouta [mountain of death];

Zel and Marzuk comfort each other as their lives are changed forever.

Genealogy (lines 574-669).

Death of Marzuk;

Horns of Gurzel pass to Zel;

Lineage and genealogy of subsequent Siwa Kings (part 1);

Relation on changes in clan technology and first development of copper tools;

Relation on peace and clan prosperity within the Siwa;

Lineage and genealogy of subsequent Siwa Kings (part 2);

Relation on changes in clan economy and first attempts at incipient cultivation;

Relation on clan decisions whether to maintain or to alter hunting-gathering customs;

Lineage and genealogy of subsequent Siwa Kings (part 3);

Relation on clan decisions to implement division of labor between hunters and growers;

Lineage and genealogy of subsequent Siwa Kings (part 4);

Valdes becomes King of Siwa;

Valdes ignores clan promise to god Zagilie and defiles the temple at Aghourmi;

God Zagilie observes Valdes's dishonorable actions.

Schism (lines 670-861).

Lineage and genealogy of subsequent Siwa Kings (part 5);

Beldn, son of Tauk, becomes King of Siwa;

Tsnet, Beldn's only son, dies unexpectedly before his initiation and test of manhood;

Beldn dies during hunting accident leaving no direct Kingship heir;

Queen Zena, Beldn's wife, grieves over the deaths of husband and son;

Tella, Beldn's brother, offers to honor clan tradition and take Zena to his hearth and bed;

Queen Zena, agrees, but because of endless love for Beldn commits suicide;

Chaos and disorder follow as adult clan members must select a new King;

Relation on clan lineages and potential hunters who might serve as King;

Two potential clan leaders identified: Tella [Beldn's brother] and Ferzin [the strongest];

Relation on the Ferzin's personality and behavior traits;

Varna [wisest elder] relates Gosla's promise and Valdes's shame to the assembled clan;

Assembled adult males make their Kingship selection;

The horns of Gurzel and Kingship of the Siwa pass to Ferzin;

Tella and his supporters fear Ferzin's retribution and make plans to leave the Siwa;

Tella challenges Ferzin to rule justly and to maintain Zagilie's laws;

Tella and Ferzin pledge honor and respect to one another at assembly of Siwan elders;

Ferzin secretly plots the death of Tella and his supporters.

Qara (lines 862-925).

Tella and his supporters depart the Siwa seeking an alternative safe haven;

Trekking eastward they pray to god Zagilie for strength, support, and guidance;

They reach the Qara, an oasis east of the Siwa filled with curious rock configurations;

Tella's band settles at the Qara;

Relation on passing seasons as Tella takes Marla as his mate;

Marla becomes pregnant but is scorned for not producing a male heir;

Marla becomes pregnant a second time and delivers a second daughter;

Marla becomes pregnant a third time and delivers a son named Rak;

The Qara settlers honor god Zagilie and pass the seasons in peace and harmony;

Two strangers—near death—arrive in the Qara seeking food and refuge.

Shame (lines 926-1017).

Daoud and Lez, the refugees, relate their story of Ferzin's brutal reign at the Siwa;

Relation on the madness of King Ferzin and desecration of Zagilie's temple at Aghourmi;

Relation on the disappearance of wild game from the Siwa;

Relation on the evil of Ferzin and his behavior as his people languished and suffered;

Relation on the imprisonment and torture of Siwan dissenters;

Relation on the trials and torture suffered by Daoud and Lez;

Relation on their ultimate banishment and desert wandering without food and water;

Adult men in Tella's band united in their pledge to depose Ferzin.

Death Duel (lines 1018-1085).

Ferzin's scouts observe the arrival of Tella's band and inform the Siwan King;

Tella and his warriors reach the Siwa and encamp below Aghourmi temple;

Tella challenges Ferzin to a hand-to-hand combat and death duel;

Relation on the death duel and the wounds suffered by each;

Relation on the Ferzin's physical strength physical superiority over Tella;

Tella falls and breaks his weapon—Ferzin lunges for the kill;

God Zagilie guides Tella's hand to a copper knife lying unnoticed on the dueling ground;

Tella guided by god Zagilie grasps the copper knife and kills Ferzin;

Ferzin is buried at the Mouta [Mountain of Death] without clan honors.

Transition (lines 1086-1169).

Tella orders Zagilie's temple at Aghourmi to be cleansed and rebuilt;

The copper knife used to slay Ferzin enshrined as a temple offering;

Death of Tella;

Tella's son Rak becomes King of Siwa and wears the Horns of Gurzel;

Lineage and genealogy of subsequent Siwa Kings (part 6);

Relation on first attempts at picture drawing and writing;

Benis tames an *o-gar-azee* and names the animal *Sal-Lukie*;

Siwan elders debate the merit and safety of tamed animals;

Tort the younger creates first bronze tools;

Relation on the first development of pottery at the Siwa;

Relation on acceptance of incipient agriculture and ultimate stabilization of food supply;

Relation on the rise of different economic activities: farmers, hunters, potters, weavers;

Relet becomes King of the Siwa;

A band of new strangers enter the Siwa.

Te-Henu (lines 1170-1321).

Arriving strangers initially appear to pose a threat to the stability of the Siwa;

During this time of crisis Whelk becomes King of the Siwa;

Whelk assembles his warriors to defend the Siwa;

Relation on the strangers, their dress, and weapons;

Strangers, calling themselves Te-Henu, advance to meet Whelk and the Siwan elders;

The Te-Henu claim to be distant relatives through the line of Marzuk's younger brother;

Siwans and Te-Henu agree to merge and form a cultural and military alliance;

The Te-Henu teach Siwans how to smelt iron and make weapons stronger than bronze;

Relation on the origin of iron weapons and early Hittu battles with Per-O King of Chem;

Relation on gradual loss of peace with expansion of Siwa/Te-Henu military ambitions;

Death of King Whelk and reign of his son Clearchus;

Clearchus rejects clan genealogy and erects a stele falsely listing clan honors;

Clearchus claims to be the greatest King who ever ruled the Siwa;

Moved by Clearchus's false claims clan members clamor for expansion beyond the Siwa;

Siwans and Te-Henu plan to attack Per-O, King of Chem, ruler of the Black Land;

Peace has vanished in the Siwa.

Battle I (lines 1322-1457).

Relation on military and political unrest in the land of Chem;

Siwa and Te-Henu soldiers attack Per-O, King of Chem near the Sea of Vanton;

Per-O Mer-En-Ptah confronts the Siwa/Te-Henu army;

Clearchus, King of Siwa, is slain in battle;

Siwa and Te-Henu forces retreat before the advancing chariots of Per-O Mer-En-Ptah;

Relation on battlefield deaths and the mutilation of the Siwa/Te-Henu dead soldiers;

Siwa/Te-Henu prisoners are presented as battle trophies to Per-O Mer-En-Ptah;

Relation on brutal deaths of prisoners demonstrating Per-O Mer-En-Ptah's power;

Siwa/Te-Henu survivors struggle to return home to the Siwa;

Zagilie's grace has left the Siwa as Aghourmi temple lies in ruins;

Relation on subsequent years of shame and dishonor that follow the defeat;

Seasons pass but shame continues to haunt the Siwa/Te-Henu;

Waves of new immigrants, Meshwesh and Temehu clans, arrive in the Siwa;

Meshwesh/Temehu clans form a military alliance with the Siwa/Te-Henu;

Calls for war and revenge against the Chemi increase;

Libu becomes King of Siwa as talk of war and vengeance increase;

Blacksmiths in the Siwa produce new and better iron weapons;

Mesher selected as war-time leader of the combined Siwa army;

Mesher's battle cry resounds across the Siwa—To the Black Land: To the Black Land!

Battle II (lines 1458-1545).

Mesher leader of the combined Siwan army attacks the Chemi homeland;

Per-O evokes protection and support of god Amon-Ra to defeat the Siwan army;

Siwans experience initial battle success over the Chemi;

Mesher relaxes his army's vigilance not expecting a Chemi dawn attack;

Ra-Horakhti, Chemi sun god, shields Per-O's army from Siwan view;

Blinded by the dawn's sun the Siwans cannot see the advancing Chemi troops;

Chemi chariots quickly cross Siwan defense lines and storm their encampment;

Havoc reigns as the Siwan army rises confused from their sleep;

Per-O User-Ma-Re Meri-Amon defeats the combined Siwan army;

Captured survivors are led away in bondage to end their lives as slaves;

Siwan leaders in defeat plead for the Per-O's mercy.

Ima (lines 1545-1625).

Per-O User-Ma-Re Meri-Amon orders a priest of Amon to survey the Siwa;

Annual tribute of food and green stones established as the price for initiating war;

Relation on the parallels between Chemi god Amon-Ra and Siwan god Gurzel;

Relation on the establishment of two oracle temples by winged messengers of Amon-Ra;

Relation on the first oracle temple constructed at Dodona, north of the Sea of Vanton;

Relation on the second oracle temple constructed on Aghourmi mount at the Siwa;

Relation on the origin of the line of Ima priestesses established at Aghourmi temple;

Relation on the roles of three priests at Aghourmi: two at present, one in the future;

Relation on identification of the Third Priest and how he will be identified and known;

Third Priest prophecy: he will arrive, depart, and his spirit will return and remain forever;

Siwans pledge to honor gods Zagilie-Amon-Ra, two as one now combined;

Relation on the return of Zagilie's grace to the Siwa.

Nep-et (lines 1626-1789).

Relation on development of economic relations between the Siwa and the Black Land;

Sen-oui, representative of Per-O, arrives at Siwa and imposes new requirements;

Green stones required as annual tribute to the god-King Per-O User-Ma-Re Meri-Amon;

Ima installed as priestess to tend the sacred fire at Aghourmi temple;

Relation on Ima's purity and prophetic visions of the future;

Relation on Ima's prophecies and their impact beyond the Siwa and Black Land;

Relation on pilgrims visiting the Siwa and Ima's prophetic messages;

Relation on priests of Chem and the introduction of Osiris worship at the Siwa;

Pilgrim arrives at Aghourmi who is ill and his disease spreads within the Siwa;

Sick pilgrim cannot be cured using traditional Siwan medical techniques;

Nep-et, Chemi physician, arrives at the Siwa and cures all who had been ill;

Nep-et suggests the Siwans identify a youth to be trained as a physician;

Nep-et relates that medical training in the Chemi House of Life will be long and difficult;

Bar-is volunteers to accompany Nep-et to the Black Land for training;

Bar-is vows to complete training and return to the Siwa;

Disturbing prophecy that Bar-is will become a physician but will not return to the Siwa.

Bar-is (lines 1790-1977).

Bar-is and Nep-et leave the Siwa and trek eastward towards the Black Land;

They pass through Qara, north of the sinking sands, and reach the *taut* [well] of Nebi;

They pass the *taut* of Qat-tara, then Mag-rah, and trek through the forest of stone trees;

Bar-is and Nep-et reach Nat-ron Valley west of the Black Land and great river;

They board a barge and sail southward past Gi-za, Men-fer, and the Plain of Death;

Bar-is marvels at the wondrous sights along the banks of the great river;

Bar-is and Nep-et arrive at We-Set where Bar-is begins training in the House of Life;

Relation on medical training in the House of Life;

Bar-is completes training and receives Sekhmet's silver bar, symbolic of his profession;

Nep-et and Bar-is make an evening visit to the temple of Per-O User-Ma-Re Meri-Amon;

The Per-O's ruined temple depicts carvings of battle scenes from the Chemi-Siwan war;

Nep-et and Bar-is view the ruined temple and ponder the past history of their peoples.

Sokkar (lines 1978-2049).

Death of Nep-et;

Nep-et's body prepared for burial in the House of Death;

Nep-et's funeral barge is readied and drifts northward towards the plain of Sokkar;

Funeral cortege arrives at Sokkar and Nep-et's coffin is carried ashore;

Cortege members reach the tomb of Im-Ho-Tep where Nep-et will be buried nearby;

Funerary party offer symbolic mummified ibis at the tomb of Im-Ho-Tep;

Relation on Nep-et's funerary rites as practiced by Chemi priests;

Relation on mourners sharing a last meal inside Nep-et's tomb;

Bar-is prays to god Im-Ho-Tep for his safe return to the Siwa.

Cambyses (lines 2050-2257).

Relation on territorial expansion of Persian King Cambyses and his army;

Persian army marches west and reaches the eastern shore of the Sea of Vanton;

Persian army turns south and west and crosses into the Black Land;

Persian army arrives at Men-Fer where Cambyses kills the sacred Apis bull;

Persian army marches south and occupies We-Set capitol of the Black Land;

Chem is conquered by the Persians;

Cambyses orders destruction of Amon-Ra's temple at Kar-Nak;

Persian rule spreads fear throughout the Black Land;

Cambyses claims to be god and orders Chemi religious monuments destroyed;

Priests of Amon-Ra are tortured to reveal hiding places of religious treasures;

Cambyses desires the green stones offered in honor and respect to Amon-Ra;

Chemi priests are tortured to reveal the source of the green stones;

Ai, an Amon-Ra priest, reveals that the green stones are mined at the Siwa;

Cambyses initiates plans for a military expedition to the Siwa;

Cambyses requires a healing priest to aid and tend his soldiers en route;

Chemi healing priests are assembled before Cambyses;

Bar-is is selected and commanded to accompany the Persian troops;

The Persian army leaves We-Set and embarks upon their overland desert trek;

Troops march northwest, reach the Blessed Isles, and establish camp within the oasis;

Bar-is learns the true mission of the Persian army and acts to prevent this evil;

Bar-is is observed mixing poison with the soldier's food and is tortured;

A sacred dove of Amon-Ra observes Bar-is's mutilation and death;

Amon-Ra's sacred dove flies to the Siwa carrying the terrible message to Ima;

The sacred dove arrives and tells Ima of the impending danger;

Siwans assemble and offer prayers for protection to Zagilie and Amon-Ra;

Persian soldiers resume their march and enter region of the Great Sand Sea;

Siwans continue to raise prayers to Zagilie and Amon-Ra;

Zagilie and Amon-Ra hear the Siwan pleas and cause the desert winds to rise;

Persian troops are engulfed in a terrible sandstorm and all perish in the Great Sand Sea.

Iskander (lines 2258-2453).

Relation on the gods of Siwa and Chem and salvation of the Siwa;

Relation on increased fame of the oracle temple at Aghourmi;

Relation on resumption of peace throughout the Siwa;

Relation on the decline of Per-O's power and political twilight of the Black Land;

Relation on the early military successes of Iskander son of Philip;

Iskander's arrival and reception in the Black Land;

Iskander reaches We-Set where he is deemed the son of god by priests of Amon-Ra;

Iskander's dreams cause shaking tremors and periods of deep trances;

Iskander decides to visit the oracle temple at the Siwa to learn his origins;

Iskander and his entourage travel north along the great river and reach the Sea of Vanton;

Iskander orders construction of a new sea-port city, one to be a center of learning;

The entourage continues west along the shore of Vanton and they reach Amon-ium;

Priests from Cyrene greet the entourage, claiming Iskander is the son of god;

The entourage turns south towards the Siwa but becomes lost in the desert;

They suffer hardships and thirst but are saved by Khumn, the Chemi ram god;

Iskander reaches the Siwa where he is greeted by priestess Ima;

Together they enter Aghourmi temple whereupon Iskander is seized by shaking tremors;

Ima rides her chair of vision, falls into a trance, and learns the origins of Iskander's birth;

Ima embraces Iskander through his shaking time;

Amon-Ra commands Iskander to remain silent regarding the mystery of his conception;

Zagilie's prophecy is recalled: *He who trembles—He will be the Third Priest;*

The entourage returns to the Great River along the track of the hero Bar-is;

Relation on Iskander's eastern military and cultural conquests;

Relation on Iskander's death at Babylon;

Relation on the transportation and return of Iskander's body to the Black Land;

Iskander's body, placed inside a coffin of gold and glass, is displayed at his new city;

Although his tomb is guarded throughout the night Iskander's body disappears.

The Third Priest (lines 2454-2465).

Description of the new dawn and the coming greatness sweeping over the Siwa;

Relation on the hymns raised in glory to honor The Third Priest;

Ima appears and shouts from Aghourmi's temple mount: He has returned!

Del-wat Imi Talta saket! [And the Third Priest dwelt among them!}

*   *   *

[End] . . .

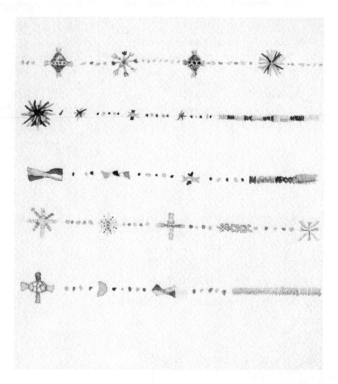

Appendix B

Maps: Locations Identified in *The Song of Siwa*

B1.   Southwestern Europe, North Africa, Nile Valley.
B2.   Siwa and Qara Oasis and Qattara Depression.
B3.   Land of Chem or Black Land [Ancient Egypt]: General Locations with Persian and Macedonian Invasion Routes.

B1: Southwestern Europe, North Africa, Nile Valley.

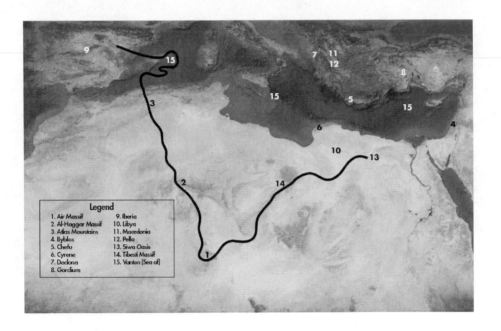

Legend

1. Air Massif
2. Al-Haggar Massif
3. Atlas Mountains
4. Byblos
5. Chefu
6. Cyrene
7. Dodona
8. Gordium
9. Iberia
10. Libya
11. Macedonia
12. Pella
13. Siwa Oasis
14. Tibesti Massif
15. Vanton [Sea of]

B2: Siwa and Qara Oases and Qattara Depression.

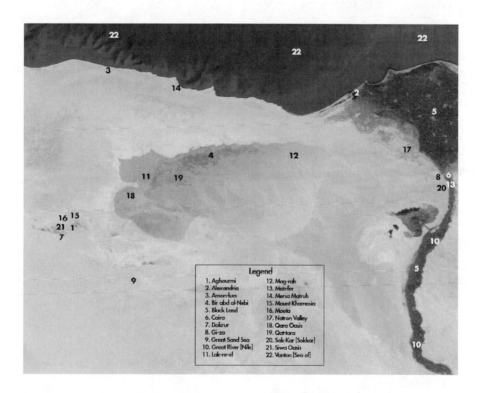

Legend
1. Aghourmi
2. Alexandria
3. Amon-lum
4. Bir abd al-Nebi
5. Black Land
6. Cairo
7. Dakrur
8. Gi-za
9. Great Sand Sea
10. Great River [Nile]
11. Lak-re-ef
12. Mag-rah
13. Meh-fer
14. Mersa Matruh
15. Mount Khamasia
16. Mavta
17. Natron Valley
18. Qara Oasis
19. Qattara
20. Sak-Kar [Sokkar]
21. Siwa Oasis
22. Vanton [Sea of]

B3: Land of Chem [Ancient Egypt]: General Locations with Persian and Macedonian Invasion Routes.

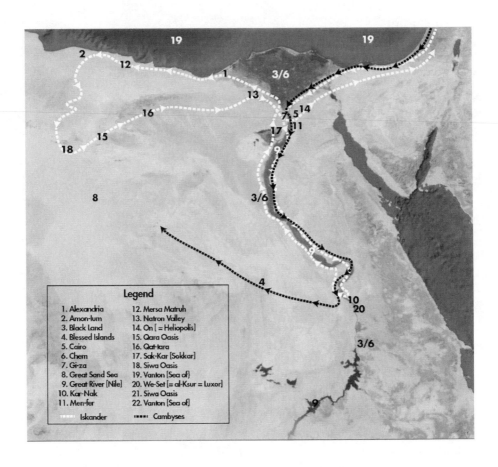

Legend

1. Alexandria	12. Mersa Matruh
2. Amon-Ium	13. Natron Valley
3. Black Land	14. On [= Heliopolis]
4. Blessed Islands	15. Qara Oasis
5. Cairo	16. Qat-tara
6. Chem	17. Sak-Kar [Sokkar]
7. Gi-za	18. Siwa Oasis
8. Great Sand Sea	19. Vanton [Sea of]
9. Great River [Nile]	20. We-Set [= al-Ksur = Luxor]
10. Kar-Nak	21. Siwa Oasis
11. Men-fer	22. Vanton [Sea of]

····· Iskander   ▪▪▪▪ Cambyses

Appendix C

Vocabulary: Persons and Terms Identified in the Epic

Presented here are the names of individuals and cultural, geographical, historical, linguistic, and religious terms mentioned by the elders during their recitation of the epic on April 15th-16th, 1965. If the spellings are inconsistent when compared to recent orthographies, I accept responsibility; these spellings are how I heard the words while transcribing the tapes. Some readers may note with interest that a number of the terms mentioned in the epic have remained through the centuries as geographical place names in contemporary north Africa and Egypt. Marzuk, the epic hero, is the designation for a prominent town located today in south-central Libya; the Siwan hero-physician, Bar-is, is honored and remembered today at a small village with a sweet-water well located in southern Khargah oasis in west central Egypt. Some argue that the name applied to Khargah oasis, itself, stems from Khargn, the father of Bar-is. Specialists will be able to identify other geographical place names that stem from various sections of the epic. Some differences in spellings between the Siwi terms for various sites in ancient and contemporary Egypt may be noted. I have maintained the Siwi spelling versions based upon sounds transcribed from the tapes made at the *mulid*.

Term	Context and Definition
aaa	Medical: name of a disease common to Chemi [Ancient Egyptian] farmers; definition uncertain, perhaps a parasite.
Aghourmi	Geography: flat-top hill east of Siwa town; site of the oracle temple; the Marzuk-Iskander festival celebrated in an open area to the west below the temple.
Ahmeht	Food: language of origin: Chemi: "wheat."
Ai	Religion: Chemi priest who collaborated with the Persian King, Cambyses.
Air	Geography: Mountainous region of the central Sahara located in central Niger.
Alexandria	Geography: Egyptian city on the Mediterranean founded by Iskander [Alexander the Great].
al-Haggar	Geography: Mountainous region of the central Sahara located in southern Algeria.
al-Taut es-Shamps	Geography: language of origin: Siwi: "well of the sun."
Amon	Religion: Chemi deity: Chief of the Chemi gods.
Amon-ium	Geography: City along the coast that marked the western political boundary of Chem.
Amon-Ra	Religion: Chemi deity: Chief of the gods. Combined form with the sun god, Ra.
Ank-Ma-Hor	Person: Chemi—noble of the 5th Dynasty buried at Sak-Kar [Saqqara].
Anubis	Religion: Chemi deity: jackal-headed god of the western lands [land of the dead].
Apis	Religion: Chemi deity: sacred bull worshiped at Men-fer [Memphis].
Ard	Person: Siwi ancient sorceress and midwife who trained Glim in women's arts.
Atlas	Geography: Mountain range of North Africa extending from modern Morocco east through Algeria into Tunisia.
Awlad Ali	Cultural Group: contemporary Egyptian Bedouin tribe. Traditional homeland west of Alexandria between the Mediterranean coast and the Qattara Depression in the Western Desert of Egypt.
Babylon	Geography: Capital of ancient Persia.

Bar-is	Person: Siwi—Son of Khargn [mother and father unknown]. Siwan youth selected by Nep-et to become a healer; subsequently murdered by Persian soldiers at the Islands of the Blessed. [NOTE: Bar-is was tortured and murdered at Khargha Oasis, a location that became a pilgrimage site after his death and eviction of the Persians. The memory of Bar-is continues to be honored at the tiny settlement and well/spring that bears his name, located in the southern district of Khargha].
Belda	Language of origin: unknown perhaps Proto-Berber; suggested translation "gazelle."
Beldn	Person: Siwi—King of Siwa; son of Tauk; mate of Zena; father of Tsnet.
Benis	Person: Siwi—youth identified in the epic as the first to tame an o-gar-azee [wild dog].
Benta	Person: Siwi—mate of King Feron.
Berber	Cultural Group: inhabitants of North Africa that occupy a geographical range from Morocco east to Qara oasis.
Berka	Language of origin: Arabic. Loan word recited in the epic: general word for "lake.
Bir abd al-Nebi	Geography: fresh water spring located along the northern edge of the Qattara Depression; name translates from Arabic as "well of the slave of the Prophet [Mohammed]."
Black Land	Geography: general descriptive term for the land of Chem [Ancient Egypt].
Blert	Person: Siwi—King of Siwa; son of Kala; father of Tola.
Blessed Islands	Geography: collective term for the oases of Khargha and Dakhla in west-central Chem [Ancient Egypt] = Islands of the Blessed.
Bouma	Language of origin: Arabic. Loan word recited in the epic; general word for "owl."
Byblos	Geography: Phoenician city located in the north of modern Lebanon.
Cairo	Geography: capital of modern Egypt. English language corruption of the Arabic, al-Kahira [The Conqueror].
Cambyses	Person: Persian—King of ancient Persia who invaded Chem, murdered the Apis bull, and ordered troops to attack Siwa oasis to gailn control of the emerald mines.
Chefu	Geography: Uncertain island kingdom in the Sea of Vanton [Mediterranean] possibly Crete (?).

Chem	Geography: Language of origin: Chemi—original name for the country now known as Ancient Egypt, also called "The Black Land."
Chnt	Person: Siwi—King of Siwa; names of his father, mate, and son not recited in the epic.
Clearchus	Person: Siwi/Libyan—King of Siwa; son of Whelk; leader of the Siwan/Tehenu military attack on the Chemi [Ancient Egyptians].
Crook and Flail	Religion: religious and political power symbols carried and displayed by Per-O, King of Chem.
Cyrene	Geography: Ancient Greek name applied to a specific Greek settlement and general geographical region of Libya.
Dakrur	Geography: mountain south of Siwa where the oasis emerald mines were located.
Dalben	Person: Siwi—King of Siwa; names of father, mate, and son not recited in the epic.
Daoud	Person: Siwi—youth (genealogy not recited in the epic); persecuted by Ferzin, who took refuge with Tella's clan at Qara oasis.
Darius	Person: Persian—King of Persia.
Darv	Person: Siwi—King of Siwa; names of father, mate, and son not recited in the epic.
Daxis	Person: Persian—One of Cambyses' generals ordered to march to Siwa oasis and take control of the emerald mines; after leaving the Islands of the Blessed, expedition members all were killed by sandstorm.
Del-wat Imi Talta saket	Language of origin: Siwi—final words shouted repeatedly at the climax of the mulid; translated as "And the Third Priest dwelt among them."
Devh	Person: Siwi—son of Taleg; full genealogy not recited in the epic.
Dezna	Person: Siwi—mate of Khal; mother of Ferzin.
Dodona	Geography: site of an important oracle temple in antiquity located in northwestern Greece; a geographical counterpart to the oracle at Siwa Oasis.
Double Crown	Religion: religious and political crown worn by Chemi Kings; symbolic of the unification of northern and southern regions of the Black Land.
Eefilan	Language of origin: Siwi—"onion"

Eli-feing	Language of origin: Siwi—"cobra" [plural noun feminine form].
Etomie	Person: Siwi—mother of Gosla.
Eye of Horus	Religion: Symbol of good fortune and protection against evil [associated with Horus the Avenger, son of Isis and Osiris].
Falil	Person: Siwi—King of Siwa; son of Valdes; father of Taz.
Fanna	Person: Siwi—King of Siwa; son of Taz; father of Tauk.
Farna	Language of origin: unknown, perhaps Proto-Berber: suggested translation, "North African leopard."
Felna	Person: Siwi/Libyan—one of four War Chiefs who declared war on the Chemi.
Fen	Person: Siwi—King of Siwa identified in the epic as ruling "twelve generations after Marzuk;" full genealogy not recited in the epic.
Ferda	Person: Siwi/Libyan—one of four War Chiefs who declared war on the Chemi.
Ferik	Person: Siwi/Libyan—one of four Siwan/Libyan War Chiefs who declared war on the Chemi.
Feron	Person: Siwi—King of Siwa; mate of Benta.
Ferzin	Person: Siwi—Son of Khal and Dezna; King of Siwa chosen after the death of Beldn and Zena; not in hereditarykingship line. Slain by Tella in death dual.
Gi-za	Geography: Pyramid plateau in northern Chem at the base of the great river [Nile] delta; royal cemetery of 4th dynasty chemi Kings and nobles [Giza].
Glim	Person: Siwi—aged sorceress and midwife who tended Gosla during the difficult delivery of twins, Zel and Zechen.
Gmena	Person: Siwi—King of Siwa; son of Tollek.
Gordium	Geography: city of west-central Anatolia in modern Turkey.
Gosla	Person: Siwi—Queen of Siwa; mate of Marzuk; parents unknown; mother of twins, Zel and Zechen.
Great Sand Sea	Geography: vast sand dune formation located in western Egypt/eastern Libya, extending south of Siwa oasis to a region northwest of Dakhla Oasis. Location where the Persian expeditionary force sent by Cambyses to attack Siwa was destroyed by sandstorm.
Great River	Geography: River running from south to north through the country of Chem [Ancient Egypt]; today known as *Nahr en-Nile* or Nile.

Gurzel	Religion: secondary god worshiped at Siwa oasis. Gurzel appeared as a horned ram, similar to the Chemi deity, Khumn. [NOTE: it has been argued by scholars that the ram's horns that appear on portrait coins of Alexander the Great are those of Gurzel, not Khumn, and that Gurzel was so honored since he was the mysterious ram god that led the Macedonians to safety at Siwa oasis after the entourage became lost in the western desert.
Hashab	Language of origin: Siwi—"branches of woven palm fronds commonly draped over graves."
Hittu	Cultural group: ethnic term recited in the epic representing an iron-age people of east/central Anatolia [Hittites]; enemies of the Chemi.
Horus (the Avenger)	Religion: Chemi deity: son of Osiris and Isis, uncle of Set; commonly depicted as a falcon.
Horus (the Elder)	Religion: Chemi deity; member of the great Pentad, brother of Osiris, Isis, Set, and Nephtys; sometimes confused with Horus the Avenger.
House of Death	Language of origin: Chemi—general translation of the term *per-mtt*, a word that designates the location where bodies were prepared for embalming.
House of Life	Language of origin: Chemi—general translation of the term *per-ank*, a word that designates the location in Chem [Ancient Egypt] where men and women studied medicine to become healers.
Iberia	Geography: Western European peninsula; location of modern Spain and Portugal. Original geographic home of the clan of Marzuk.
Ifadel	Language of origin: Arabic—"please."
Ik-ful	Language of origin: Arabic—"open" (verb command form).
Ima	Person: Siwi—maiden and first Priestess who served in the temple dedicated to Amon-Ra/Zagilie at Aghourmi. [NOTE: name passed down through multiple generations of Priestesses. The epic suggests that the Priestess who greeted Iskander (Alexander the Great) was the 16th Ima].
Im-Ho-Tep	Person: Chemi—physician-architect of the 3rd Dynasty; considered the father of ancient medicine. His tomb at Sak-kara [Saqqara] is located north of the step pyramid of King Zo-ser [Zoser] and served as a pilgrimage site for more than 4,000 years.

In-sha Allah	Language of origin: Arabic—"if God permits."
Ipix	Language of origin: Siwi—bird with rich plumage [perhaps an egret].
Islands of the Blessed	Geography: general translation of terms that refer to the desert oases in west-central Chem, specifically, Khargha and Dakhla. [See also: Blessed Islands].
Isis	Religion: Chemi deity: member of the great Pentad, sister to Osiris, Set, Nephtys, and Horus the Elder; wife of Osiris and mother of "Horus the Avenger."
Iskander	Person: Macedonian—regional spelling and pronunciation at Siwa oasis for "Alexander the Great."
Izm	Language of origin: Siwi—Identification uncertain, probably an antelope species.
Ka	Religion: Chemi religious/death concept: one aspect of the human soul.
Ka-Gm-Ni	Person: Chemi—noble of the 5th Dynasty, buried at Sak-Kar [Saqqara].
Ka-hr-ka	Language of origin: Chemi—fourth month of the annual calendar.
Kala	Person: Siwi—King of Siwa; son of Mela; father of Blert.
Kar-Nak	Geography: Chemi language spelling variant for the great temple of Karnak located at ancient Wes-Et [modern Luxor].
Kel-et	Person: Siwi—King of Siwa, son of Zel.
Khal	Person: Siwi—mate of Dezna; father of Ferzin [full genealogy not recited in the Siwan epic].
Khargn	Person: Siwi—respected elder and father of Bar-is. [NOTE: so respected was Khargn that his name has continued to be honored into the 21st century where it serves as the linguistic basis for the name of Khargha Oasis in western Egypt].
Khell	Language of origin: Siwi—a type of ancient mask used during male initiation rites by Marzuk's clan.
Khumn	Religion: Chemi deity: ram-headed god with curled horns. [NOTE: sometimes confused and/or equated with Gurzel].
Kpr	Language of origin: Siwi—"copper."
Kuftan	Language of origin: Arabic—long sleeve robe worn by boys and men.
Lak-re-ef	Geography: sand dune formations located between Siwa and Qara oases.

Lez	Person: Siwi—youth persecuted by Ferzin who took refuge with Tella's clan at Qara oasis [genealogy not recited in the epic].
Libu	Person: Siwi—King of Siwa [genealogy not recited in the epic]; identified as war chief during the 2nd Siwan/Libyan war against the Chemi.
Libya	Geography: Greek language term for the country west of Chem, named derived from Libu, King of Siwa.
Lubki	Language of Origin: Siwi—a lightly alcoholic beverage prepared from palm tree sap. [NOTE: despite its alcohol content, *lubki* is permitted to Muslims and sometimes served to oasis visitors.
Mag-rah	Geography: small oasis and sand dune area at the northeastern edge of the Qattara Depression.
Malah	Language of origin: Arabic—loan word recited in the epic; a watery mixture of salt and unidentified bitter herbs applied during torture to open wounds in order to cause severe pain.
Margunah	Language of origin: Siwi—"decorative basket."
Marla	Person: Siwi—mate of Tella; mother of Rak and two daughters [names not recited in the epic].
Meru-Ka-Ra	Person: Chemi—noble of the 5th Dynasty, buried at Sak-Kar [Saqqara].
Marzuk	Person: Siwi—central heroic figure of the epic's early passages; King of Siwa, mate of Gosla, father of Zel and Zechen.
Mela	Person: Siwi—King of Siwa; son of Peno; father of Kala.
Men-fer	Geography: "City of the White Walls." [NOTE: this is a spelling variant of the Greek word, Memphis; Men-fer was the first capital of Chem and administrative center of the united upper and lower regions along the great river [Nile].
Mer-En-Ptah	Person: Chemi—King of Chem; presumed son of Ramses II.
Mersa Matruh	Geography: Egyptian coastal town along the Mediterranean near the border with Libya; northern terminus of the track to Siwa oasis.
Mesher	Person: Siwi—Primary Siwan/Libyan War Chief who declared war on the Chemi.
Meshwesh	Cultural group: Libyan tribe who aligned politically and culturally with the Siwans; original homeland located northwest of Siwa oasis along the Mediterranean coast.

Midas	Person: Lydian—King of Lydia in western Anatolia.
Mount Khamasia	Geography: Mountain located along the eastern border of Siwa oasis.
Mouta	Geography: small mount located north of the central settlement at Siwa; traditional burial place for Siwan Kings and notables; term derived from an Arabic loan word meaning "death."
Muchan	Language of origin: Siwi—uncertain, perhaps a root vegetable (?)
Mulid	Language of origin: Arabic—"festival."
Nabis	Person: Siwi—One of four Siwan/Libyan War Chiefs who declared war on the Chemi; father of Tolla.
Natron	Geography: desiccating salt used to embalm the dead in Chem [Ancient Egypt]; mined at Natron Valley.
Natron Valley	Geography: area correlated with modern day Wadi Natron, located along the west-central edge of the Nile delta.
Nebi [Taut of]	Language of origin: Siwi/Arabic combination of loan words recited in the epic: translates as "well of the Prophet." Known in the 21st century in the Arabic language as Bir abd-al-Nebi [Well of the Slave of the Prophet].
Nefer	Person: Chemi—wife of Ramose, who traveled to Siwa seeking advice from Priestess Ima.
Nep-et	Person: Chemi—esteemed healer; teacher and companion of Bar-is.
Nepthys	Religion: Chemi deity: member of the great Pentad, sister to Osiris, Isis, Seth, and Horus the Elder; sister/wife of Seth.
Nut	Religion: Chemi deity: sky goddess and mother of the great pentad (Osiris, Isis, Set, Nepthys, and Horus the Elder).
O-gar-azee	Language of origin: Siwi—"wild dog."
On	Geography: Chemi city located at the apex of the great river delta [Nile]; known in the 21st century by its Greek name, Heliopolis [city of the sun].
Ork	Person: Siwi—King of Siwa [full genealogy not recited in the Siwan epic].
Osiris	Religion: Chemi deity: member of the great Pentad, sister/wife of Isis, brother to Set, Nepthys, and Horus the Elder.
Pella	Geography: city of Macedonia; birthplace of Iskander [Alexander the Great].
Pelo	Person: Siwi—Siwan/Libyan war chief who declared war on the Chemi.

Peno	Person: Siwi—King of Siwa; son of Rak; father of Mela.
Per-O	Language of origin: Chemi—term translates as "great house"; King and ruler of the Black Land [Ancient Egypt].
Philip of Macedon	Person: Macedonian—traditional, earthly father of Iskander [Alexander the Great].
Plen	Person: Siwi—King of Siwa; son of Tola.
Prnex	Language of origin: Siwi—"ostrich."
Qara	Geography: oasis east of Siwa. Name stems from the Proto-Berber language meaning: "unusual rock formations." Qara oasis served as a haven for Tella and his followers.
Qat-tara	Geography: geological feature of the western desert of Egypt, between Qara and Mag-rah oases; a below sea-level depression and region of salt marshes and "sinking sands."
Ra	Religion: Chemi deity—god of the sun.
Ra-Harakhte	Religion: Chemi deity—sun god of the eastern horizon [dawn].
Rak	Person: Siwi—son of Tella and Marla; King of Siwa; father of Peno.
Ramose	Person: Chemi—husband of Nefer.
Ramses II	Person: Chemi—King of Chem; presumed father of Mer-En-Ptah.
Ramses III	Person: Chemi—King of Chem; presumed son of Mer-En-Ptah. Religious/warrior name: User-Ma-Re Meri-Amon.
Razallah	Language of origin: Siwi—"evil eye."
Relet	Person: Siwi—King of Siwa; uncertain parentage; ruled after Plen; father of Whelk.
Sak-Kar	Geography: Early Siwi variant of the word Saqqara, the royal cemetery area west of Memphis. [See also Sokkar].
Sal-Lukie	Language of origin: Siwi—"swiftest wind." [NOTE: name subsequently applied to all tamed o-gar-azee (wild dogs)].
Sekhmet	Religion: Chemi deity: lion-headed goddess of desiccating wind; associated with healing.
Sen-oui	Person: Chemi—scribe sent by Per-O to monitor and administer the oasis after the Siwan/Libyan defeat.
Set	Religion: Chemi deity—member of the great Pentad, brother to Osiris, Isis, Horus the Elder, and sister/wife of Nepthys.
Shu	Religion: Chemi deity—god of air and father of Nut [Sky].

Siwa	Geography: Oasis and central focus of the epic. Located in the western desert of Egypt near the border with Libya. Origin of term unknown, perhaps Proto-Berber: suggested translation "home" or "place of safety."
Sokkar	Geography: Siwi pronunciation of Saqqara; royal cemetery west of Memphis. Term sometimes used in the context of "land of the dead." [See also Sak-Kar]
Taleg	Person: Siwi—young man of Marzuk's clan and father of Devh; genealogy not recited in the epic.
Talgo	Person: Siwi—younger brother of Marzuk; founder of the Te-Henu clan that settled along the coast in Libya.
Tamzooah	Language of origin: Siwi—"wild grain."
Tarik	Person: Phoenician—King of Byblos who traveled to Siwa to seek information from the Priestess Ima.
Tasher	Person: Siwan/Libyan war chief who declared war on the Chemi.
Tasou-tet	Language of origin: Siwi—palm tree logs that form part of the super-structure atop Siwan graves.
Tauk	Person: Siwi—King of Siwa; son of Fanna; father of Beldn and Tella.
Taut	Language of origin: Siwi—"well or spring of fresh water."
Taz	Person: Siwi—King of Siwa; son of Falil; father of Fanna.
Teglast	Language of origin: Siwi—pestle used to grind herbs and grains.
Te-Henu	Cultural group: Libyan tribe: homeland northwest of Siwa oasis near the coast. As recited in the epic the Te-Henu are linked by blood to Marzuk's clan.
Tella	Person: Siwi—son of Tauk; brother of Beldn; mate of Marla; father of Rak; defeated Ferzin in death duel to become King of Siwa.
Telt	Person: Siwan/Libyan War Chief who declared war on the Chemi.
Temehu	Cultural group: Libyan tribe: homeland located northwest of Siwa oasis near the coast. [NOTE: not related by blood to Marzuk's clan].
Thala	Person: Siwi—elderly woman of Marzuk's clan; among the first named persons in the Siwa epic; genealogy not recited in the epic.
Thelt	Person: Siwi—King of Marzuk's clan two generations after the death of Zel; full genealogy not recited in the epic.

Themer	Person: Siwan/Libyan War Chief who declared war on the Chemi, son of Wrmr.
Theno	Person: Siwi—member of Marzuk's clan; inventor of bellows for smelting ore; genealogy not recited in the epic.
Tibesti	Geography: mountainous upland region in the Sahara near southwestern Libya and northeastern Chad.
Tola	Person: Siwi—King of Siwa; father of Plen [NOTE: not to be confused with Tolla—names of the two were pronounced differently during recitation of the epic].
Tolla	Person: Siwan/Libyan War Chief who declared war on the Chemi, son of Nabis [NOTE: this individual should not be confused with Tola—names of the two persons were pronounced differently—doubling of the "ll" sound—during recitation of the epic].
Tollek	Person: Siwi—King of Siwa; father of Gmena; full genealogy not recited in the epic.
Tort	Person: Siwi—clan member who discovered a new way to smelt copper; genealogy not recited in the epic.
Tsnet	Person: Siwi—Son of Beldn; died before his initiation and appointment as King of Siwa.
Tzesia	Language of origin: Siwi—"cicadas."
Un-Is	Person: Chemi—King of the 5th Dynasty.
User-Ma-Re Meri-Amon	Person: Chemi—King of Chem. Religious/warrior name of Ramses III
Valdes	Person: Siwi—King of Siwa; father of Falil; full genealogy not recited in the epic.
Vanton [Sea of]	Language of origin: Proto-Berber?—"Mediterranean Sea."
Varna	Person: Siwi—respected elder and sage of the Siwa clan.
Vedro	Language of origin: Proto-Berber (?)—perhaps "large antelope."
We-Set	Geography: Chemi capital city during the reign of Ramses II, Mer-En-Ptah, and Ramses III [known in the 21st century as Luxor].
Whelk	Person: Siwi—King of Siwa; son of Relet; father of Clearchus.
Wrmr	Person: Siwan/Libyan—Military leader of the Te-Henu; father of Themer.
Yardin	Language of origin: Siwi—"wheat."
Yatouss	Language of origin: Siwi: wooden torture implement used for anal penetration of prisoners.

Zagilie	Religion: Siwi—Proto-Berber name of god worshiped by the clan of Marzuk and his descendants.
Za'qikla	Language of origin: Siwi—"Assembly." [NOTE: in the sense used during transliteration of the epic, it specifically means words repeated by those gathered to hear the recitation of the epic].
Zechen	Person: Siwi—son of Marzuk and Gosla, twin brother of Zel; killed during initiation rites.
Zeitun	Language of origin: Arabic—loan word used in the epic—"olive."
Zel	Person: Siwi—King of Siwa; son of Marzuk and Gosla, twin brother of Zechen; father of Kel-et.
Zelda	Language of origin: Proto-Berber—"wild zebra."
Zena	Person: Siwi—Queen of Siwa; mate of Beldn; mother of Tsnet.
Zo-ser	Person: Chemi—King of the 3rd Dynasty.

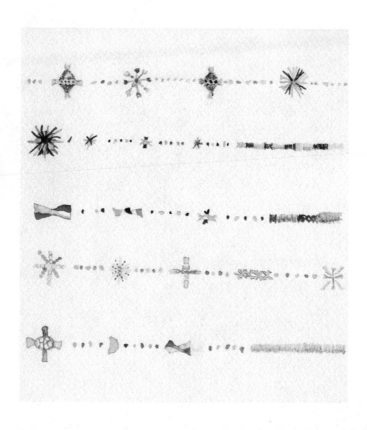

Appendix D

Selected Original Ancient Accounts: Events Identified in *The Song of Siwa*

Defeat of the Siwan/Libyan Army by Merenptah Son of Ramses II, King of Chem:

[Siwan/Libyan army routed] . . . *Their advanced columns they left behind them, their feet made no stand, but fled. Their archers threw down their bows, and the heart of their fleet ones was weary with marching. They loosed their water skins and threw them to the ground, their . . . [section missing] . . . were taken and thrown out* [Breadsted, J. H., 1865-1935. *Ancient Records of Egypt.* Vol. 3. Section 608, pp. 260].

[Siwan/Libyan war-leader disgraced] . . . *The wretched, fallen chief of Libya, fled by favor of night alone, with no plume upon his head, his two feet failed. His women were taken before his face, the grain of his supplies was plundered, and he had no water in the skin to keep him alive. The face of his brothers was hostile to slay him, one fought another among his leaders. Their camp was burned and made a roast, all his possessions were food for the troops. Then he arrived in his country, he was the complaint of every one in his land. Ashamed, he bowed himself down, an evil fate removed his plume. They all spoke against him, among the inhabitants of his city: "He is in the power of the gods, the lords of Memphis, the lord of Egypt has cursed his name, Meryey, the abomination of Memphis, from son to son of his family, forever. Binre-Meriamon is in pursuit of his children; Merneptah-Hotephirma is appointed to be his fate.* [Breadsted, J. H., 1865-1935. *Ancient Records of Egypt.* Vol. 3. Section 609-610, pp. 260-362].

[Siwan/Libyan soldiers mutilated] . . . *Children of the wretched fallen chief of Libya whose uncircumcised phalli were carried off. Children of chiefs, brothers of the wretched, fallen chief of Libya, carried off as the . . .* [section missing] . . . *of Libya, slain, whose phalli were carried off—6,200 men . . .* [section missing] . . . *of the families of Libya, slain, whose phalli were carried off—200 men . . .* [section missing] . . . *the fallen chief of Libya whose hands were carried off—2,201 men* [Breadstead, J. H., 1865-1935. *Ancient Records of Egypt*, Vol. 3. Section 601, p. 255].

[Siwan-Libyan army destroyed] . . . *Those who reached my border are desolated, their seed is not. The Libyans and the Seped are wasted, their seed is not. The fire has penetrated us, our seed is not . . . Their cities are made ashes, wasted, desolated; their seed is not* [Breadsted, J. H. 1865-1935. *Ancient Records of Egypt.* Vol. 3. Section 604, p. 258].

Defeat of the Siwan/Libyan Army by Ramses III, King of Chem:

Behold, I will inform you of other things, done in Egypt since my reign. The Libyans and the Meshwesh were dwelling in Egypt, having plundered the cities of the western shore, from Memphis to Kerben. They had reached the great river on both its banks. They it was who plundered the cities of Egwowe during very many years, while they were in Egypt. Behold, I destroyed them, slain at one time. I laid low the Meshwesh, the Libyans, the Esbet, the Keykesh, the Shai, the Hes and the Beken; they were overthrown in their blood and made heaps. I turned them back from trampling the border of Egypt. I carried away those whom my sword spared, as numerous captives, pinioned like birds before my horses, their wives and their children, by the ten-thousand, their cattle in number like hundred-thousand. I settled their leaders in strongholds in my name. I gave to them captains of archers, and chief men of the tribes, branded and made into slaves impressed with my name;

their wives and children were made likewise. I led their cattle into the house of Amon; they were made into herds, forever [Breadsted, J. H. 1965-1935. *Ancient Records of Egypt.* Vol. 4, Section 405, p. 229].

Foundation of the Oracle Temple at Ammon [Siwa]:

This was what I heard from the priests at Thebes; at Dodona, however, the women who deliver the oracles relate the matter as follows: "Two black doves flew away from Egyptian Thebes, and while one directed its flight to Libya, the other came to them. She alighted on an oak, and sitting there began to speak with a human voice, and told them that on the spot where she was, there should henceforth be an oracle of Jove. They understood the announcement to be from heaven, so they set to work at once and erected the shrine. The dove which flew to Libya bade the Libyans to establish there the oracle of Ammon." This likewise is an oracle of Jupiter [Herodotus, *The Histories.* Translated by George Rawlinson. Book II].

Cambyses at Memphis: Death of the Apis Bull:

About the time when Cambyses arrived at Memphis, Apis appeared to the Egyptians. Now Apis is the god whom the Greeks call Epaphus. As soon as he appeared, straightway all the Egyptians arrayed themselves in their gayest garments, and fell to feasting and jollity: which when Cambyses saw, making sure that these rejoicings were on account of his own ill success, he called before him the officers who had charge of Memphis, and demanded of them—"Why, when he was in Memphis before, the Egyptians had done nothing of this kind, but waited until now, when he had returned with the loss of so many of his troops?" The officers made answer, "That one of their gods had appeared to them, a god who at long intervals of time had been accustomed to show himself in Egypt—and that always on his appearance the whole of Egypt feasted and kept jubilee." When Cambyses heard this, he told them that they lied, and as liars he condemned them all to suffer death [Herodotus, *The Histories.* Translated by George Rawlinson. Book III].

When they were dead, he called the priests to his presence, and questioning them received the same answer; whereupon he observed, "That he would soon know whether a tame god had really come to dwell in Egypt"—and straightway, without another word, he bade them bring Apis to him. So they went out from his presence to fetch the god. Now this Apis, or Epaphus, is the calf of a cow which is never afterwards able to bear young. The Egyptians say that fire comes down from heaven upon the cow, which thereupon conceives Apis. The calf which is so called has the following marks: He is black, with a square spot of white upon his forehead, and on his back the figure of an eagle; the hairs in his tail are double, and there is a beetle upon his tongue [Herodotus, *The Histories.* Translated by George Rawlinson. Book III].

When the priests returned bringing Apis with them, Cambyses, like the harebrained person that he was, drew his dagger, and aimed at the belly of the animal, but missed his mark, and stabbed him in the thigh. Then he laughed, and said thus to the priests: "Oh! Blockheads [sic] *and think ye that gods become like this, of flesh and blood, and sensible to steel? A fit god indeed for Egyptians, such a one! But it shall cost you dear that you have made me your laughing-stock." When he had so spoken, he ordered those whose business it was to scourge the priests, and if they found any of the Egyptians keeping festival to put them to death. Thus was the feast stopped throughout the land of Egypt, and the priests suffered punishment. Apis, wounded in the thigh, lay some time pining in the temple; at last he died of his wound, and the priests buried him secretly without the knowledge of Cambyses* [Herodotus, *The Histories.* Translated by George Rawlinson. Book III].

Army of Cambyses Lost in the Great Sand Sea:

Cambyses took counsel with himself, and planned three expeditions. One was against the Carthaginians, another against the Ammonians, and a third against the long-lived Ethiopians, who dwelt in that part of Libya which borders upon the southern sea . . . The men sent to attack the Ammonians, started from Thebes, having guides with them, and may be clearly traced as far as the city Oasis, which is inhabited by Samians, said to be of the tribe Aeschrionia. The place is distant from Thebes seven days' journey across the sand, and is called in our tongue "the Island of the Blessed." Thus far the army is known to have made its way; but thenceforth nothing is to be heard of them, except what the Ammonians, and those who get their knowledge from them, report. It is certain they neither reached the Ammonians, nor even came back to Egypt. Further than this, the Ammonians relate as follows: That the Persians set forth from Oasis across the sand, and had reached about half way between that place and themselves when, as they were at their midday meal, a wind arose from the south, strong and deadly, bringing with it vast columns of whirling sand, which entirely covered up the troops and caused them wholly to disappear. Thus, according to the Ammonians, did it fare with this army [Herodotus, *The Histories.* Translated by George Rawlinson. Book III].

Foundation of the City of Alexandria:

Alexander—rose up and went to Pharos, which, at that time, was an island lying a little above the Canopic mouth of the river Nile, though it has now been joined to the mainland by a mole. As soon as he saw the commodious situation of the place, it being a long neck of land, stretching like an isthmus between large lagoons and shallow waters on one side and the sea on the other, the latter at the end of it making a spacious harbor, he said, Homer, besides his other excellences, was a very good architect, and ordered the plan of a city to be drawn out answerable to the place. To do which, for want of chalk, the soil being black, they laid out their lines with flour, taking in a pretty large compass of ground in a semi-circular figure, and drawing into the inside of the circumference equal straight lines from each end, thus giving it something of the form of a cloak or cape; while he was pleasing himself with his design, on a sudden an infinite number of great birds of several kinds, rising like a black cloud out of the river and the lake, devoured every morsel of the flour that had been used in setting out the lines; at which omen even Alexander himself was troubled, till the augurs restored his confidence again by telling him it was a sign the city he was about to build would not only abound in all things within itself, but also be the nurse and feeder of many nations [Plutarch. *Parallel Lives. Alexander.* Translated by John Dryden].

Alexander's March to the Oasis of Ammon [Siwa]:

He commanded the workmen to proceed [with the construction of Alexandria], *while he went to visit the temple of Ammon. This was a long and painful, and, in two respects, a dangerous journey; first, if they should lose their provision of water, as for several days none could be obtained; and, secondly, if a violent south wind should rise upon them, while they were travelling through the wide extent of deep sands, as it is said to have done when Cambyses led his army that way, blowing the sand together in heaps, and raising, as it were, the whole desert like a sea upon them, till fifty thousand were swallowed up and destroyed by it. All these difficulties were weighed and represented to him; but Alexander was not easily to be diverted from anything he was bent upon. For fortune having hitherto seconded him in his designs, made him resolute and firm in his opinions, and the boldness of his temper raised a sort of passion in him for surmounting difficulties; as if it were not enough to be always victorious in the field, unless places and seasons and nature herself submitted to him. In this journey, the relief and assistance the gods afforded him in his distresses were more remarkable, and obtained greater belief than the oracles he received afterwards, which, however, were valued and credited the more on account of those occurrences. For first, plentiful rains that fell preserved them from any fear of perishing by drought, and, allaying the extreme dryness of the sand, which now became moist and firm to travel on, cleared and purified the air. Besides this, when they were out of their way, and were wandering up and down, because the marks which were wont to direct the guides were disordered and lost, they were set right again by some ravens, which flew before them when on their march, and waited for them when they lingered and fell behind; and the greatest miracle, as Callisthenes tells us, was that if any of the company went astray in the night, they never ceased croaking and making a noise till by that means they had brought them into the right way again* [Plutarch. *Parallel Lives. Alexander.* Translated by John Dryden].

Alexander was seized by an ardent desire to visit Ammon in Libya, partly in order to consult the god, because the oracle of Ammon was said to be exact in its information, and Perseus and Heracles were said to have consulted it, the former when he was dispatched [sic] by Polydectes against the Gorgons, and the latter, when he visited Antaeus in Libya and Busiri in Egypt. Alexander was also partly urged by a desire of emulating Perseus and Heracles, from both of whom he traced his descent. He also deduced his pedigree from Ammon, just as the legends traced that of Heracles and Perseus to Zeus. Accordingly he made the expedition to Ammon with the design of learning his own origin more certainly, or at least that he might be able to say that he had learned it. According to Aristobulus, he advanced along the sea-shore to Paraetonium through a country which was a desert, but not destitute of water, a distance of about 1,600 stades. Thence he turned into the interior, where the oracle of Ammon was located. The route is desert, and most of it is sand and destitute of water. But there was a copious supply of rain for Alexander, a thing which was attributed to the influence of the deity; as was also the following occurrence. Whenever a south wind blows in that district, it heaps up the sand upon the route far and wide, rendering the tracks of the road invisible, so that it is impossible to discover where one ought to direct one's course in the sand, just as if one were at sea; for there are no landmarks along the road, neither mountain anywhere, nor tree, nor permanent hill standing erect, by which travelers might be able to form a conjecture of the right course, as sailors do by the stars. Consequently, Alexander's army lost the way, and even the guides were in doubt about the course to take. Ptolemy, soil of Lagus, says that two serpents went in front of the army, uttering a voice, and Alexander ordered the guides to follow them, trusting in the divine portent. He says too that they showed the way to the oracle and back again. But Aristobulus, whose account is generally admitted as correct, says that two ravens flew in front of the army, and that these acted as Alexander's guides. I am able to assert with confidence that some divine assistance was afforded him for probability also coincides with the supposition but the discrepancies in the details of the various narratives have deprived the story of certainty [Arrian. Anabasis. Book 3:3].

Alexander's Arrival at the Oasis of Ammon [Siwa]:

Having passed through the wilderness, they came to the place where the high priest, at the first salutation, bade Alexander welcome from his father Ammon. And being asked by him whether any of his father's murderers had escaped punishment, he charged him to speak with more respect, since his was not a mortal father. Then Alexander, changing his expression, desired to know of him if any of those who murdered Philip were yet unpunished, and further concerning dominion, whether the empire of the world was reserved for him? This, the god answered, he should obtain, and that Philip's death was fully revenged, which gave him so much satisfaction that he made splendid offerings to Jupiter, and gave the priests very rich presents. This is what most authors write concerning the oracles [Plutarch. *Parallel Lives. Alexander.* Translated by John Dryden].

Alexander's Visit to the Oracle Temple and Return March to the Nile Valley:

The place where the temple of Ammon is located is entirely surrounded by a desert of far-stretching sand, which is destitute of water. The fertile spot in the midst of this desert is not extensive; for where it stretches into its greater expanse, it is only about forty stades broad. It is full of cultivated trees, olives and palms; and it is the only place in those parts which is refreshed with dew. A spring also rises from it, quite unlike all the other springs which issue from the earth. For at mid-day the water is cold to the taste, and still more so to the touch, as cold as cold can be. But when the sun has sunk into the west, it gets warmer, and from the evening it keeps on growing warmer until midnight, when it reaches the warmest point. After midnight it goes on getting gradually colder: at day-break it is already cold; but at midday it reaches the coldest point. Every day it undergoes these alternate changes in regular succession. In this place also natural salt is procured by digging, and certain of the priests of Ammon convey quantities of it into Egypt. For whenever they set out for Egypt they put it into little boxes plaited out of palm, and carry it as a present to the King, or some other great man. The grains of this salt are large some of them *being even longer than three fingers' breadth; and it is clear like crystal. The Egyptians and others who are respectful to the deity, use this salt in their sacrifices, as it is clearer than that which is procured from the sea. Alexander then was struck with wonder at the place, and consulted the oracle of the god. Having heard what was agreeable to his wishes, as he himself said, he set out on the journey back to Egypt by the same route, according to the statement of Aristobulus; but according to that of Ptolemy, son of Lagus, he took another road, leading straight to Memphis* [Arrian. *Anabasis.* Book 3:4].*

Alexander's Death, Return of His Body to Alexandria, and His Coffin:

When Philocles was archon in Athens, Gaius Sulpicius and Gaius Aelius were elected consuls in Rome. In this year Arrhidaeus, who had been placed in charge of bringing home the body of Alexander, having completed the vehicle on which the royal body was to be carried, was making preparations for the journey. Since the structure that had been made ready, being worthy of the glory of Alexander, not only surpassed all others in cost—it had been constructed at the expense of many talents—but was also famous for the excellence of its workmanship, I believe that it is well to describe it [Diodorus Siculus. *Library of History.* 18:26:1-2].

First they prepared a coffin of the proper size for the body, made of hammered gold, and the space about the body they filled with spices such as could make the body sweet smelling and incorruptible. Upon this chest there had been placed a cover of gold, matching it to a nicely, and fitting about its upper rim. Over this was laid a magnificent purple robe embroidered with gold, beside which they placed the arms of the deceased, wishing the design of the whole to be in harmony with his accomplishments. Then they set up next to it the covered carriage that was to carry it. At the top of the carriage was built a vault of gold, eight cubits wide and twelve long, covered with overlapping scales set with precious stones. Beneath the roof all along the work was a rectangular cornice of gold, from which projected heads of goat-stags in high relief. Gold rings two palms broad were suspended from these, and through the rings there ran a festive garland beautifully decorated in bright colors of all kinds. At the ends there were tassels of network suspending large bells, so that any who were approaching heard the sound from a great distance. On each corner of the vault on each side was a golden figure of Victory holding a trophy. The colonnade that supported the vault was of gold with Ionic capitals. Within the colonnade was a golden net, made of cords the thickness of a finger, which carried four long painted tablets, their ends adjoining, each equal in length to a side of the colonnade [Diodorus Siculus. *Library of History.* 18:26:3-3-6].

On the first of these tablets was a chariot ornamented with work in relief, and sitting in it was Alexander holding a very splendid scepter in his hands. About the King were groups of armed attendants, one of Macedonians, a second of Persians of the bodyguard, and armed soldiers in front of them. The second tablet showed the elephants arrayed for war who followed the bodyguard. They carried Indian mahouts in front with Macedonians fully armed in their regular equipment behind them. The third tablet showed troops of cavalry as if in formation for battle; and the fourth, ships made ready for naval combat. Beside the entrance to the chamber there were golden lions with eyes turned toward those who would enter. There was a golden acanthus stretching little by little up the center of each column from below to the capital. Above the chamber in the middle of the top under the open sky there was a purple banner blazoned with a golden olive wreath of great size, and when the sun cast upon it its rays, it sent forth such a bright and vibrant gleam that from a great distance it appeared like a flash of lightning [Diodorus Siculus. *Library of History.* 18:27:1-2].

The body of the chariot beneath the covered chamber had two axles upon which turned four Persian wheels, the naves and spokes of which were gilded, but the part that bore upon the ground was of iron. The projecting parts of the axle were made of gold in the form of lion heads, each holding a spear in its teeth. Along the middle of their length the axles had a bearing ingeniously fitted to the middle of the chamber in such a way that, thanks to it, the chamber could remain undisturbed by shocks from rough places. There were four poles, and to each of them were fastened four teams with four mules harnessed in each team, so that in all there were sixty-four mules, selected for their strength and size. Each of them was crowned with a gilded crown, each had a golden bell hanging by either cheek, and about their necks were collars set with precious stones [Diodorus Siculus. *Library of History.* 18:27:3-5].

In this way the carriage was constructed and ornamented, and it appeared more magnificent when seen than when described. Because of its widespread fame it drew together many spectators; for from every city into which it came the whole people went forth to meet it and again escorted it on its way out, not becoming sated with the pleasure of beholding it. To correspond to this magnificence, it was accompanied by a crowd of roadmenders [sic] and mechanics, and also by soldiers sent to escort it [Diodorus Siculus. *Library of History.* 18:28:1-2].

When Arrhidaeus had spent nearly two years in making ready this work, he brought the body of the King from Babylon to Egypt Ptolemy, moreover, doing honor to Alexander, went to meet it with an army as far as Syria, and, receiving the body, deemed it worthy of the greatest consideration. He decided for the present not to send it to Ammon, but to entomb it in the city that had been founded by Alexander himself, which lacked little of being the most renowned of the cities of the inhabited earth. There he prepared a precinct worthy the glory of Alexander in size and construction. Entombing him in this and honoring him with sacrifices such as are paid to demigods and with magnificent games he won fair requital not only from men but also from the gods [Diodorus Siculus. *Library of History.* 18:28:2-4].

Appendix E

Selected Readings

Late Pleistocene-Holocene Geology and Archaeology: Southwestern Europe, North Africa, Sahara Regions, North Coast of Egypt, and Siwa Oasis:

Cline, W. 1928. Notes on the Origin of the People of Siwa and Gara. *Man.* 28(February): 24-25.

Close, A. E. and F. Wendorf. 1987. *Prehistory of Arid North Africa. Essays in Honor of Fred Wendorf.* Dallas, Texas: Southern Methodist University Press.

Hassan, F. A. 1978. Archaeological Explorations of the Siwa Oasis Region, Egypt. *Current Anthropology.* 19(1):146-148.

Hassan, F. A., and G. T. Gross. 1987. *Resources and Subsistence during the early Holocene at Siwa Oasis, Northern Egypt.* [Dallas]: Southern Methodist University Press.

Kuhlmann, K. P. 2001. Gleanings from the Texts in the Sanctuary of Amun at Aghurmi (Siwa Oasis). *Mitteilungen-Deutschen Archaologischen Instituts Abteilung, Kairo.* 57: 187-204.

Mercuri, A., L. Sadori, and P. U. Qilero. 2011. Mediterranean and North-African Cultural Adaptations to Mid-Holocene Environmental and Climatic Changes. *The Holocene.* 21(1): 189-206.

Mueller, U., H. Pliett, K. P. Kuhlmann, and F. Wenzel. 2002. Structural Preservation of the Temple of the Oracle in Siwa Oasis, Egypt. *Conservation and Management of Archaeological Sites.* Vol. 5, Part 4: 215.

Salem, M. J., and M. T. Busrewil. 1980. *The Geology of Libya.* London, England: Academic Press.

Salman, A. A. B. 1984. *Bibliography of Geology and Related Sciences, Concerning Western Desert, Egypt (1732-1984).* Cairo, Egypt: Egyptian Geological Consulting Office.

Sampsell, B. M. 2003. *A Traveler's Guide to the Geology of Egypt.* Cairo, Egypt: American university in Cairo Press.

Steindorff, G. 1904. Eine archäologische reise durch die libysche wüste zur Amonsoase Siwe. [Berlin: no publisher].

Tawadros, E. 2011. *Geology of North Africa.* Boca Raton, Florida.: CRC Press.

Thomas, E. S. 1926. A Comparison of Drawings from Ancient Egypt, Libya, and the South Spanish Caves. *Journal of the Anthropological Institute of Great Britain and Ireland.* 56: 385-394.

Archaeology: Siwa Oasis:

Dzierzykray-Rogalski, T. 1984. The Cult of Amon in the Siwa Oasis (Egypt). *Africana Bulletin, Warsaw University,* Volume 42.

Fakhry, A. 1950. *The Oasis of Siwa: Its Customs, History and Monuments.* Cairo, Egypt: Wadi el-Nil Press.

Fakhry, A. 1978. Archaeological Explorations of the Siwa Oasis Region, Egypt. *Current Anthropology.* 19(1): 146-148.

Fakhry, A. 1990. *Siwa Oasis.* Cairo Egypt: American University in Cairo Press.

Hassan, F. A. 1978. Archaeological Explorations of the Siwa Oasis Region, Egypt. *Current Anthropology.* 19(1): 146-148.

Hassan, F. A., and G. T. Gross. 1987. *Resources and Subsistence during the early Holocene at Siwa Oasis, Northern Egypt.* Dallas, Texas: Southern Methodist University Press.

Kuhlmann, K. P. 1988. Das Ammoneion: Archäologie, Geschichte und Kultpraxis des Orakels von Siwa. *Archäologische Veröffentlichungen,* Vol. 75. Mainz am Rhein: P. von Zabern.

Mueller, U., H. Pliett, K. P. Kuhlmann, and F. Wenzel. 2002. Structural Preservation of the Temple of the Oracle in Siwa Oasis, Egypt. *Conservation and Management of Archaeological Sites.* Vol. 5, Part 4.

Parke, H. W. 1967. *The Oracles of Zeus: Dodona, Olympia, Ammon.* Oxford: Blackwell.

Rovero, L., U. Tonietti, F. Fratini, and S. Rescic. 2012. The Salt Architecture in Siwa Oasis—Egypt (XII-XX Centuries). *Construction and Building Materials.* 23(7): 2492-2503.

Siwan-Libyan-Egyptian Conflicts:

El-Mosalamy, A. H. S. 1984. Libyco-Berber Relations with Ancient Egypt. The Tehenu in Egyptian Records. *Libya Antiqua.UNESCO Symposium, Paris,* 16-18 January, 1984. pp. 61-68.

Forbes, R. H. 1942. Egyptian-Libyan Borderlands. *Geographical Review.* 32(2): 294-302.

Hamblin, W. J. 2006. *Warfare in the Ancient Near East to 1600 BC: Holy Warriors at the Dawn of History.* London, England: Routledge.

Hyland, A. 2002. *The Horse in the Ancient World.* Westport, Connecticut: Praeger.

Naylor, P. C. 2009. *North Africa: A History from Antiquity to the Present.* Austin, Texas: University of Texas Press.

Partridge, R. B. 2002. *Fighting Pharaohs: Weapons and Warfare in Ancient Egypt.* Manchester, England: Peartree Publishers.

Pemberton, D. 2005. *Atlas of Ancient Egypt.* New York, New York: Harry N. Abrams in association with the British Museum.

Spalinger, A. 2005. *War in Ancient Egypt. The New Kingdom.* Oxford, England: Blackwell Publishing.

Cambyses and Destruction of the Persian Troops:

Mallet, D. 1979. *Relations of the Ancient Greeks with Late Pharaonic and Persian Egypt: From the Conquest by Cambyses to Alexander the Great 525-331 B.C.* Chicago, Illinois: Ares Publishing House.

Rashbrook, S., I. Denyer, and C. Ledger. 2002. *The Lost Army of King Cambyses.* VHS Video, Channel Four (Great Britain). London: Channel Four Television Corporation.

Sussman, P. 2003. *The Lost Army of Cambyses.* New York, New York: Thomas Dunne Books.

Alexander's Visit to Siwa:

Curnow, T. 2004. *The Oracles of the Ancient World.* London, England: Duckworth.

Herve, H. F. C. 1929. *Review of Ulrich Wilken: Alexanders Zug iln die Oase Siwa.* Berlin: Weidemann.

Lamer, H. 1930. *Alexanders Zug in die oase Siwa.* Leipzig: Deitrich.

Lehmann-Haupt, C. F. 1930. Zu Alexanders Zug in de Oase Siwa. *Klio: Beiträge zur alten Geschichte.* 24(1930). 169-190.

Manfredi, V. M. and G. Minghini. 2010. *Le tombeau d'Alexandre le Grand: l'énigme.* [Paris]: Lattès.

Milne, J. G. 1929. *Alexander and Ammon.* London, England: Macmillan.

Schlange-Schoningen, H. 1996. Alexandria-Memphis-Siwa: wo liegt Alexander der Grosse begraben? *Antike Welt.* 27(2):109-119.

Souvaltzi, L. 2002. *The Tomb of Alexander the Great at the Siwa Oasis: The History of the Archaeological Excavation and Its Political Background.* Athens, Greece: Georgiadis.

Weber, T. 1995. Jungste Spekulationen um das Grab Alexanders des Grossen. *Antike Welt.* 26(1): 80a.

Wilcken, U. 1928. *Alexanders Zug in die Oase Siwa.* Berlin: Verlag der Akademie der wissenschaften.

19th and 20th Century Descriptions of Siwa and Qara Oases:

Aldumairy, Abd el-Azia el-Rahman. 2005. *Siwa. Past and Present.* Alexandria, Egypt: Privately Published.

Belgrave, C. D. [1923?]. *Siwa: the Oasis of Jupiter Ammon.* Boston, Massachusetts: Small and Maynard.

Belgrave, C. D.1923. Review of Siwa. The Oasis of Jupiter Ammon. *Journal of the Royal African Society.* Vol. 22(87):255-256.

Bliss, F. 1981. *Kulturwandel in der Oase Siwa (Ägypten): Geschichte, Wirtschaft und Kultur einer ägyptischen Oase seit dem Mittelalter.* Bon: Arbeitskreis für Entwicklungspolitik.

Blottière, A. 1992. *L'oasis: Siwa.* Paris: Quai Voltaire.

Butt, M. T., and A. R. Cury. 1936? *Mersa-Matruh: How to See It, Including Siwa and the Western Desert: With a Vivid Account of War Operations of 1915-17.* Cairo: World-Wide Publications.

Dun, T. I. 1933. *From Cairo to Siwa: Across the Libyan Desert with Armoured Cars.* Cairo: E. & R. Schindler.

Hassanein Bey, A. M. 1924. Crossing the Untraversed Libyan Desert. *National Geographic Magazine.* 46(3): 233-278.

Helmi, I. 1982. Siwa to Wadi Natroun by Camel: Five Researchers Travel an Old Caravan Route. *Cairo Today.* 3(12) [December issue].

Hoskins, G. A. 1837. *Visit to the Great Oasis of the Libyan Desert: With an Account, Ancient and Modern, of the Oasis of Amun, and the Other Oases Now Under the Domination of the Pasha of Egypt.* London, England: Longman, Rees, Orme, Brown, Green, & Longman.

Jennings-Bramly, W. 1897. A Journey to Siwa in September and October, 1896. *The Geographical Journal.* 10(6): 597-608.

Jennings-Bramly, W. 1902. A Journey from Farafra to Siwa, 1898. *The Geographical Journal.* 19(1):73-75.

Kennedy Shaw, W. B. 1954. *Long Range Desert Group: The Story of its Work in Libya 1940-1943.* London: Collins.

Khalil, M. 1933. *Report on the Mission of the Research Institute, Public Health Department, and the Faculty of Medicine, Cairo, to Siwa Oasis, in January 1933, for the Study of Parasitic Infections, Malaria, and Diphtheria.* Cairo: Government Press.

Rikli, M., G. Karsten, and H. Schenck. 1929. *Durch die Marmarica zur Oase Siwa.* Jena: Fischer.

Scholz, J. M. A. 1822. *Travels in the Countries between Alexandria and Paraetonium, the Lybian Desert, Siwa, Egypt, Palestine, and Syria, in 1821.* London: Sir Richard Phillips and Co.

Simpson, G. E. 1929. *The Heart of Libya: The Siwa Oasis, It's People, Customs and Sport.* London, England: H. F. & G. Witherby.

Stanley, C. V. B. 1912. The Oasis of Siwa. *Journal of the Royal African Society.* 11(43): 290-324.

Walker, W. S. An Outline of Modern Exploration in the Oasis of Siwa. *The Geographical Journal.* 57(1): 29-34.

White, A. S. 1984. *From Sphinx to Oracle: through the Libyan Desert to the Oasis of Jupiter Ammon.* London, England: Darf Publishers.

Siwa Oasis: Culture, Handicrafts, and Everyday Life:

'Abd Allan, M. M. 1917. Siwan Customs. Peabody Museum, *African Department. Harvard African Studies.* Volume 1. Boston, Massachusetts: Harvard University Press.

Badrawi, R. A., O. Hikal, K. Shokryh. 2011. *Siwa: Legends & Lifestyles in the Egyptian Sahara.* Hong Kong, China: Haven Books.

Basset, R. 1890. Le dialecte de Syouah. *Publications de l'École des lettres d'Alger. Bulletin de corresopndance Africaine.* Volume 5. Paris: E. Leroux.

Bliss, F. 1981. Islamischer Volksglaube in Der Oase Siwa (Ägypten). *De Welt des Islams.* 21(1): 9-29.

Bliss, F. 1998. *Siwa: die Oase des Sonnengottes. Leben in einer ägyptischen Oase vom Mittelalter bis in die Gegenwart.* Bonn: PAS.

Bliss, F., and M. Weissenberger. 1983. Jewelry from the Siwa Oasis. *Ornament.* 6(4):6-11, 42-44.

Blottière, A., and C. Clement. 2000. *Siwa: The Oasis.* Alexandria, Egypt: Harpocrates.

Burton, R. P., and M. Symes. 1996. *Egyptian Rural Settlement Patterns: Analysis and Interpretation of the Spacial Characteristics of Siwa Oasis.* Manchester: University of Manchester Press.

Lewis, M. P. 2009. *Siwa: A Language of Egypt.* Ethnologue: Languages of the World (16th Edition). SIL International (*www. sil.org*).

Malim, F. 2001. *Oasis Siwa: From the Inside. Traditions, Customs and Magic.* Privately Published.

Maugham, R. 1950. *Journey to Siwa.* New York: Harcourt and Brace.

Murray, G. W. 1945. The Customs of Siwa. From an Anonymous Arabic MS. *Man.* 45(July-August): 82-84.

Rovero, L., U. Tonietti, F. Fratini, and S. Rescic. 2013. The Salt Architecture in Siwa Oasis, Egypt (XII-XX Centuries). *Construction and Building Materials.* 23(7):2492-2503.

Schieneri, P. W. 1980. Female Jewelry from Siwa Oasis (Egypt). *Acta Ethnographica Academiae Scientiarum Hungaricae.* 29 (1-2): 167-180.

Schiffer, B. 1936. *Die Oase Siwa und ihre Musik.* Dissertation, University of Berlin. Bottrop: W. Postberg.

Schieneri, P. W. 1980. Female Jewelry from Siwa Oasis (Egypt): A Concise Survey. *Acta Ethnographical Academiae Scientiarum Hungaricae.* 29:167-180.

Souryai, S. S. 2001. Social Control in the Oasis of Siwa: A Study in Natural Justice and Conflict Resolution. *International Criminal Justice Review.* 11(1): 82-103.

Stein, L. and W. Rusch. 1978. *Die Oase Siwa: unter Berbern u. Beduinen d. Libyschen Wuste.* Leipzig: Brockhaus, VEB.

Vivian, C. 1991. *Siwa Oasis: Its History, Sites and Crafts.* Maadi, Egypt: International Publications.

Walker, W. S. 1921. *The Siwi Language: A Short Grammar of the Siwi Language, with a Map and Ten Appendices, Including a Brief Account of the Customs, etc., of the Siwani, Together with a Description of the Oasis of Siwa.* London, England: K. Paul, Trench, Trubner & Co.

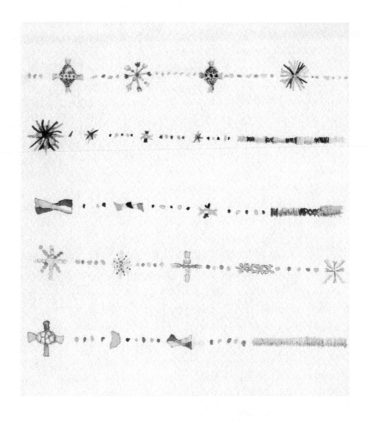